A CURSE OF STONE AND FIRE

A B BLOOM

For Lana

HISTORY...

The Romans invaded Albion in the First Century AD. Conquering and enslaving; they were horrified by the brutish Gaelic clans which they encountered.

The annexe of Albion complete; they turned their attention to Caledonia. There they met a force unlike any they had seen before. The wild Celtic clans forced back the encroachment of foreigners withstanding the onslaught under which they found themselves.

The Druids removed themselves from history around the same time as the Roman arrival. Wild and savage, they led their people: their women powerful, their ways dark and wicked.

There were those who wanted the power they controlled... those who would stop at nothing to get it and wait however long it took to find it.

1

The car hit a pothole and bounced, the back wheels lifting from the worn tarmac.

I woke with a start, blinking into daylight. The remnants of my unexpected dream faded away as I stared in surprise through the window of the sedan. Those eyes... I rubbed at my head, my fingers catching in the knotted tangle of my hair. How many times had I dreamed of those dark eyes? They seemed to chase me every time I fell asleep. I shouldn't have been dozing anyway, but the flight from the States was zapping the life out of me.

"Could we slow down a bit?" I leant forward, my hand gripping onto the leather upholstery of the passenger seat. "I dislike sitting in the back." The guy in the chauffeur cap had insisted; he'd almost pushed me in through the rear door of the black car and now my fingers gripped the headrest like my life depended on it.

He wasn't one to chat—or even answer—but I didn't let the fact deter me. "How far is it to Fire Stone?"

His eyes met mine in the rear-view. Beneath bushy grey

brows his eyes were surprisingly bright. I couldn't deter-
mine his age. Was he old with mysteriously large eyebrows?
Or was he young with unfortunate facial hair growth?
Maybe the mystery would never be solved.

"Not far." His reply was monosyllabic. Not for the first
time.

I sat up further, straining against the seatbelt cutting
into my neck. "But, where is that exactly? I've never been to
England before. Is it in a town? A village? Is it by the sea?"
Fire Stone could be anywhere. All I knew was it was the last
place in the world I wanted to go, and yet here I was stuck
in the back of a car which was seemingly being driven by a
rally driver.

We hurtled another corner as his massive brows
crimped together—he wasn't even looking at the road. "Aye,
and you still haven't. This is Scotland."

"Same thing though, right? It's all the same island?" My
hands slipped against leather as we took another corner at
high speed around a right turn.

His glare was dagger ridden.

"Is that why the airport was so small?" I asked.

Another glare.

"Is that why there weren't many lights? It's not exactly
London, is it? Where was that place I landed?"

"Aberdeen."

I held back a giggle. *Aberdeeeeen.* "Is that the capital of
Scotland?"

"No."

"What is then?" If I kept hammering away he might
finally succumb and talk to me.

"Edinburgh."

I giggled again unable to resist. *Edinbuuuuurgh.*

"Let me get this straight. Scotland is its own country, even though it's part of a tiny island you could fit into America ten times over?"

"Hmph."

This was almost a full conversation so I launched into my next question. "And where's my aunt? Why hasn't she come to get me?" Flushing a little, I glanced out the window at the green countryside. "I kind of figured she would, seeing as I haven't seen a family member for ten years."

There was a pause—I filled it. "Sorry, I'm asking so many questions." I risked releasing a hand from my tight grip on the headrest to brush hair out of my eyes. "Only, I haven't spoken to anyone since I left Queens, well apart from the air stewards, but they couldn't stop and chat long."

"Your aunt is away." Five syllables. We were bonding.

Okay, then. "So, she isn't going to be there when I arrive?" The little alarm which had been ringing at the back of my mind, deep within my worry-box, jangled again.

"No."

"And where is 'Fire Stone', exactly?" If I keep asking, someone may answer.

"Not far."

I groaned and slumped back against the seat, my head dropping back. "Sure," I muttered. "Not far."

Realising I wasn't going to get any answers, I rummaged in the ancient, leather overnight duffle bag on the seat next to mine. I pulled at the letter and smoothed it against my leg, easing the creases with my hands. The paper was thick and expensive, the cursive script elegant and sweeping. An invitation from a great aunt, it told me to come to *Fire Stone* as I was now under her care.

This of course was highly ironic.

*Dear Maeve, news of your plight has reached my ears...
My travels take me far and wide, and your situation has been
long coming to my attention. As is proper in situations such
as these, I have set the wheels in motion to become your legal
guardian. With no remaining relatives in the United States, I
expect you to travel to meet me here and to enrol at Fire
Stone where you shall continue your education. All expenses
shall be met by my own purse.*

Her own purse? Who spoke like that?

And. *Hell, no.*

My cheeks flamed every time I thought about it.
Although, obviously my refusal to enrol was short-lived—I
was in a limousine on a journey to nowhere.

Being an orphan was an obstructive conversation stop-
per. People found out and reacted in the same way. First
there was the awkward pause. Then there was the *I'm so
sorry I didn't know.* Then followed the bit where I waved
my hand and told them that it was all okay and not to worry.
I felt worse for making someone feel bad which was ironic
considering it was me who was parentless.

Fire Stone.

I smelled the paper, searching some long-forgotten scent
I'd been chasing all my life and then folded the embossed
paper with care along the creases, popping it back into the
bag. As I ran my hands down the length of my jeans, I
breathed in and out through my nose. Palms sweating and
unable to sit still, this would go down as one of the most
uncomfortable car journeys of my life.

"It's my first time in a limo." I leant forward again,
unable to resist the urge to talk.

My answer was another stern look from under those
bushy brows in the rear-view.

"Is this how my aunt commutes?" I glanced out of the

window at the swollen clouds. "It seems fancy." Sliding my butt along the leather seat again I wrapped my arms around the headrest of the passenger chair. "She must be someone pretty important to have a chauffeur."

No answer.

"If she's away who will be there to look after me?" It was a joke. I didn't need looking after. At just eighteen and largely self-sufficient, I was more than capable. But it was fun to wind the silent driver up by asking inane questions.

"Everything is taken care of."

"Everything?" That warning bell jangled again. "Why did she write and ask me to come if she isn't going to be here?"

He didn't answer, which was no surprise. Instead, he nodded his head at a giant set of wrought-iron gates. I craned my neck to see the top. Bronze motifs supplemented black iron-work, and leaves and flowers ornately wound their rigid stems around the posts of the gates in intricate patterns. "Whoa." The car slowed to a halt giving me a close up of the impressive entrance.

My jaw dropped as the gates swung open without a sound. A small signpost with black, bold lettering on a white board simply stated Fire Stone.

"Are we here?" I bounced on the leather seat causing the bushy brows to furrow together. "Hey, I'm excited! I've never left New York before. This is awesome." No one would believe it back home.

I blocked all thoughts of home from my mind as we cruised up a wide sweeping drive. The driveway turned a broad corner before ending in a horseshoe in front of a crumbling building covered in dark creeping ivy. "What on earth?"

I blinked as a handful of children walked past the limo.

Only a couple tried to peer in through the tinted glass. My excitement at my first leg of my new life cooled. "This is awful." I shrunk back into the leather upholstery.

It was a school, which was bad enough in the grand scheme of things, but worse, it was what movies portrayed as a proper 'English' school. The kids milling around were all dressed in identical navy blazers with navy and silver ties. Girls and boys alike.

"I am not going in there." I folded my arms. I wasn't given to childish dramatics—having grown up real quick at the age of seven but... "I sure as hell didn't fly all this way to go to some school with a bunch of snobs wearing a uniform." I'd tried to research Fire Stone—it didn't exist in internet land. There was no reference to it at all. "I'm going to be eighteen in a few days," I don't know why I continued to speak to the chauffeur, his lack of conversation didn't give me hope of any answers. "This is all completely unnecessary."

The pit of my tummy clenched and dropped, and I palmed a sticky hand through my hair, strands of red tangling into my fingers.

"Mrs Cox is inside," he said, completely ignoring my protests.

"Mrs Cox?" *Who the hell is Mrs Cox?*

"She's waiting for you." The chauffeur hesitated, his gaze meeting mine in the mirror. "It's not that bad; this is a good school." From under the eyebrows I caught a glimmer of sympathy.

"But I don't need to go to school. My education is over, done, finished."

"I'm sure Mrs Cox will explain." The driver dropped his gaze and opened his door, walking around to my side of the dark sedan and pulling on the handle of my door. I'd been by myself for ten years—I'd faced almost everything by myself with only passing temporary carers to guide or support me. But right there and then I wanted to hide under the smooth floor mat of the car and never surface into fresh air. A crowd was gathering which only made my sweaty-palm syndrome worse.

"I don't want her to explain. Could you take me back to the airport please?" I frowned back out of the window. "That building looks like it's about to fall down."

"Out you get, lassie." The nameless driver had hardly been verbose on the drive here, but his tone softened as he called me lassie, and somehow my legs responded, jerking to life and stepping out of the car.

I was grabbing the universe containing duffel from the backseat when the scrunch of heels on gravel pricked at my ears. Swallowing, I straightened and turned. The woman in front of me was so small I had to lower my expectant gaze, and then lower it some more to find her face. With a hooked nose, lips dipped with a pronounced V, and round eyes, she reminded me of a sparrow bobbing for seed. Quick bright eyes focused on mine. The grey of her hair made her eyes seem more silver though up closer they were a pale blue. Tiny and birdlike, her fingers jerked towards me in greeting and I shook her hand, wondering how she maintained such a ferocious grip when she owned a wrist that looked like it would snap if knocked too hard. "Miss Adams. I'm Mrs Cox. I hope you had a good journey."

My gaze swept over to the chauffeur standing stiffly by the door. "Illuminating," I told her.

She chuckled. "Jeffries has been with us a long time."

I attacked my chance, shouldering my bag. "Forgive me

for being rude, but I really don't need to be here, not that I know where here is? *Jeffries*." I arched an eyebrow at my silent driver. "Has been vague. But really, I don't need to go to school, I've finished. I can just meet my aunt, say hi, and be on my way."

The birdlike face of Mrs Cox cracked into a smile. "On your way where? Maybe when you see what we have on offer, you will change your mind about being finished with the education system. All we ask is you give the lessons and our wonderful school a try." Her words took the wind out of the sails of my argument. Where was I planning on going? I had no money, nothing to fall back and rely on. She waved a scrawny arm at the arched wooden door. "Now let's get you some tea and toast. You like jam, dearie?" She clucked much like a mother hen, albeit a tiny, scrawny hen. "Of course you do," she answered for me. "Everyone likes jam."

I shrugged not knowing what she was talking about.

"You must be exhausted." Taking my bag with single-handed ease, she thrust it at Jeffries. "Take that to Dorm B," she told him, grabbing my elbow and wheeling me towards the uneven stone steps leading up to the worn brick building.

On closer inspection, Fire Stone resembled a castle made from crumbly, hard cheddar; where a large chunk could fall off at any moment. With bricks the colour of a sunset on a glorious day, it looked as if it had stood the test of time and now hung on by the last brick in its foundations. The dark ivy, so drab and opposing from the distance of the sweeping driveway was actually lit with little white flowers. "Beautiful, isn't it?" said Mrs Cox. I nodded, meeting her gaze. I'd need to remind myself she wasn't called Mrs Bird. I could already feel that mistake scorching my tongue.

"Where is *it* exactly? I know we are in Scotland, but that's it. Jeffries was tight with information."

I needed to process the fact I'd left New York—even rundown Queens—and flown for hours, all to be delivered to a school which was built within a dilapidated castle. I'd save stewing on that for later. I was here now, my plane ticket paid for by my mysterious aunt. I needed to find out all the information to hand before I decided on my plan of action. The only way to do that was to embrace Mrs Cox's offer of tea, toast, and jam. Whatever jam was.

"Oh, you mean jelly." I took the offered dainty, white china cup. "Strawberry jelly." I'd been offered an array of flavours but had settled on the safe sounding strawberry.

"Jelly? You Americans do like to muddle everything up."

I prickled and picked my shoulders up from their slouch. "That's a bit strong; it's only a noun for something that goes on bread."

Mrs Cox had already made me seriously pissed when she'd held out a silver tray and nodded at it with intent. "Cell phone, please. No students have phones here." I'd watched her for a moment in silent disbelief before realizing she wasn't joking and unwillingly handed my cell over. I'd put up with her nonsense while I carried on investigating the place, but then I'd want my cell straight back. Thank you very much.

Mrs Cox's room was a comfortable study: all dark green leather, and wood panelling. Hanging from one wall was a tapestry my eyes couldn't stop staring at. Giant stones were stitched in silver and grey. Around them wove sparks of magical fireflies in vibrant gold. It was stunning. If she saw me looking she didn't comment.

The crackle of the fire sparked, and I inched my leg towards it. Heat lapped up the surface of my exposed skin. It was May; springtime in Queens. I'd travelled in shorts and a zipped hoodie. The inside of Fire Stone hadn't received the Spring memo and was chilled down to its dark grey bricks.

"You will adapt to our ways, I'm sure." She offered me a secure smile and perched her glasses back onto the bridge of her nose.

"I don't need to adapt. I haven't said I'm staying yet. According to my aunt's letter, the only reason I'm enrolled is because I'm under eighteen." Mrs Cox offered me a tight smile.

"Of course." Her sharp gaze searched my face—what she was looking for I didn't know. "Your birthday is soon, you must be excited to be eighteen?"

Excited? I wanted to tell her I wasn't five and didn't get excited about birthdays anymore, but I kept quiet and shrugged. A birthday was another day of the year.

She carried on, ignoring my silence and shoulder shrugging. "Your ancestors came from these lands, Maeve. Aye, I'm sure your blood will soon remember." She nodded to herself and seemed to drift into deep thought.

"Really?" I quizzed her. "I don't know anything about my ancestors. I didn't even know I had an aunt until a month ago."

Her expression closed like the slam of a book. "Well, I'm sure everything will unfold in good time."

"What will?" I leant closer. "And where is my aunt?

Surely she should be here after asking me to come all this way?"

"She will come soon." A flicker sparked in her round eyes, and a shiver crawled up my spine.

"Why do I feel like I'm an imposition? Why make me come to an awful school in a different country and then not be here?"

Mrs Cox trilled a laugh. "Don't be silly, Maeve. And you need to do what's best for you."

"People call me Mae." I corrected her. My blood boiled and simmered, my glare icy. "People who know me call me Mae." I added.

Her eyes narrowed. "Aye, course they do." She muttered something under her breath, but I couldn't catch what it was. Her accent was thick, almost unintelligible.

I settled back with a defeated sigh and sipped at the scorching tea held within a tiny cup. I couldn't fit my finger through the delicate handle, so I gripped it from underneath. Mrs Cox frowned at my lack of etiquette. "I still can't believe my aunt isn't here to greet me." I pushed further. "I haven't seen a family member in ten years—didn't even know I had one—surely she should be here..." I trailed off when it was clear Mrs Cox wasn't going to sway under my sob story approach.

She smoothed her skirt with her hands. "It's a regrettable inconvenience," she waved her fingers in the air and smiled. "But, I assure you, I am here, and I will do everything I can to help you settle into your new life. I want you to feel at home here."

"New life? This is only a visit." A tight band wound its way around my rib cage. "I can't stay. I won't stay." I could have added that there was no way on this side of forever I was going to stay in the school once I'd turned eighteen. I shook my head. I should never have come. Never opened that damn letter. Should have run away.

"Do you have somewhere else to be?"

I hesitated. Of course I had nowhere else to be. It was the fundamental story of my life. "Well, no. I've been put in homes I haven't wanted before; it's part of being a child orphan."

"You aren't here because you are an orphan, Mae." She paused for a moment, her sharpened gaze sweeping over me. "You are here because you're family and this is where you belong."

"I've never belonged anywhere," I muttered, but I was running out of steam. "I'm tired, the flight is catching up with me." Exhaustion washed over me and my legs and arms began to pull with a heavy ache, like I'd been running a marathon, or been finally defeated in the tenth round of a fight.

"You will be happy here." It was a statement I wasn't meant to argue with. Mrs Cox gave me a nod of her head and a small smile. "Come, you're tired." I bit my tongue from a fast and loose response—they'd got me in trouble before. "Let's get you settled."

I humphed in response, but she dismissed our conversation and motioned for me to place my tiny cup on the tray of tea things she'd had laid out on a small card table by another member of staff. I drained the cup and clattered it down onto its saucer. "Sorry," I mumbled, when she frowned at my heavy-handedness with her fine china.

"Not to worry, dearie. It's just an old family heirloom, a mere trifle, I suppose." She shrugged, waving her hand and opening the door. The room had become toasty and warm from the fire in the grate, but a chill blasted with the opening of the door, much like a stiff north-westerly wind.

I shivered and rubbed at the goose bumps spreading along my skin as we marched along the dim corridors. It seemed schools were damp in Scotland although I wasn't surprised. Occasionally, as we wound through the maze of low-ceilinged passages, I sought a glimpse out of a lead window. Although the glass was aged and yellowed in some places, it didn't detract from, or improve, the dismal view outside. Heavy thunderous curtains of wet gloom obscured any view further than a couple of measly feet. There must be scenery out there somewhere—it was just invisible from the inside of the stone walls.

"Does it always rain?" I ran to keep up with Mrs Cox's short legs. She moved with surprising speed and I resembled an elephant crashing through foliage in her wake.

"Sometimes it shines." She shouldered on, barely glancing in my direction.

"The sun?"

"The sun, the moon, sometimes the stars."

"Okay." I didn't have any other answer to give. The crumbling building wasn't giving off warm and cosy inviting vibes—I didn't think walking around at night would be at the top of my to-do list.

"So, how many students do you have?"

"Just two hundred." Her gaze slipped to the side, running over me. "Your uniform will be ready; your aunt has it all arranged."

Uniform? Was she batshit crazy?

"Has she? Yet she's not here. How did she know what size I would be?" I filed away the thought of only two hundred students. That was the same amount of one single year in my last school. Mrs Cox didn't answer how my aunt knew my size despite never laying eyes on me. And honestly, I couldn't even think about it—I flew all this way to meet an aunt I didn't know—*was I crazy?*

We came to a stop outside a dark wooden door. "This is the girls wing. There are house rules, but I'm sure you will be brought up to speed by your new friends.

I liked her optimism. I wasn't going to tell her I wouldn't be here long enough to make friends.

"Is it a dorm?" I asked.

Mrs Cox pushed on the door, and a shiver of apprehension stalked its way along my spine. Nothing about this was anywhere near my expectations, and my expectations had been minimal, to say the least. Of course, when I'd found out I was flying to Britain, I'd considered the prospect I'd maybe bump into a royal prince and fall madly in love, living out a wondrous and unexpected fairy tale. But, honestly, what girl didn't have those dreams?

I glanced up and down the dark hallway and said goodbye to the fantasy. There'd be no princes here, of that I was sure.

The door creaked open with a Hitchcock groan. "You have your own room. Some girls share, others have singles, it all depends."

"On what?" We faced yet another new corridor, equally dark, but this one was lined with symmetrical oak doors on either side.

Mrs Cox shrugged. "Money."

"I don't have any." No point pretending otherwise.

She blinked at me from behind thick lenses. "You have family."

The conversation was cut short by a door further down the hallway flinging open. A girl with insanely wild, curly hair, barged through the door, her navy and silver tie askew, and a piece of toast hanging out of her mouth. Her shirt gaped at the buttons, the tail sticking out where she hadn't pushed it into the waistband of her skirt. When her gaze landed on Mrs Cox, her face dropped in shock, her skin paling to that of an albino polar bear.

"Late again, Philomena?" Mrs Cox's heels clacked across the flagstone floor. The girl, Philomena, nodded and opened her mouth as Mrs Cox removed the dangling slice of toast.

"Sorry, Mrs Cox, my alarm didn't go off again." Philomena dropped her gaze. She was earthy and messy, her colouring rich: with her dark hair and olive skin, and she towered over Mrs Cox's small neat figure. It was like looking at David and Goliath, and Goliath was quaking in his boots.

"Never mind," snapped Mrs Cox, with a curtness which made the wild-haired girl and me both wince. "Actually." She patted her hair back into place. It was as if standing in front of the whirlwind mess of Philomena had ruffled her own smooth appearance. It hadn't. "You can take Maeve here under your wing."

"Mae," I interjected. "People call me Mae."

Philomena stared at me, her eyes wide like saucers. "You're the American."

"Yep, last I checked."

"This is too exciting! A real-life American."

"There are quite a few of us, we aren't a rare breed."

Philomena grinned and grabbed at my arm. "Never had one here before. This is going to be wicked."

Mrs Cox coughed, and when I ripped my eyes away from the girl clutching my arm, I found a frown of disapproval etched into the older woman's face. "I believe, Miss

Potts, you mean fun. This will be fun. I doubt very much there will be anything wicked about it.

Philomena dropped her gaze. "No, Mrs Cox. You are right, Mrs Cox."

"Good." The woman straightened, still only coming up to Philomena's shoulder. "I shall leave you to give Maeve a tour and then you can take her to class."

"Class? Already?"

"Of course. I said you shall attend classes while you are here."

"But I've finished my education."

Mrs Cox raised an arched eyebrow. "So you said earlier, but have you really? Where's the harm in taking a few classes while you're here?"

I went to open my mouth to tell her yes, that I'd achieved all I could achieve with the limited funds I had available, but she turned on her heel. "Room thirteen please, Philomena." She waved a dismissal over her shoulders, her heels already clacking and echoing away.

Philomena gasped and turned to me. I met her gaze. She was wildly attractive in an unkempt, unfinished kind of way, as if she'd been pulled from the earth and crafted from nature's own gifts. Next to her, I was a bland, nondescript, pale imitation of young womanhood. "You're in room thirteen." She actually quaked as she said the number out loud.

"What's wrong with that?"

Philomena giggled, but it held an awkward key, like a musical instrument out of tune. "Nothing, nothing at all. Come on, let's get you settled and then you can tell me all about being American."

I chuckled, the sound surprising me. "I think it's the same as being British."

She smiled, and I grinned back. "No, you have to make it sound better. Lie if you have to."

"Okay. You asked for it though." We both turned to the room with 'Thirteen' nailed in brass figures to the wooden door.

I ignored the shiver and the inch of anxiety in my stomach. It was a room. What was the worst that could happen?

2

In the time it had taken for me to drink tea and eat a soggy piece of toast with Mrs Cox, Jeffries had delivered my duffle to room thirteen. The duffle sat, an island of familiarity on the bed, in a sea of the unknown.

"Just to warn you, Alicia will want to have a party to celebrate your arrival, and numerous house rules will be broken." Philomena broke my attention, and I turned. "So, if you aren't into rule breaking, then I'd probably feign a headache."

"I'm not opposed to rule breaking." I smiled, trying to make it an honest friendly smile and not a scary 'please be my friend' grimace. "But I am tired. I've been travelling for —" I couldn't remember how long I'd been travelling for. "What time is it now?"

"Nine. I'm late for class. Although, thanks to you I'll be let off—this time."

"Glad to be of service." I stepped further into the room. Sparse furniture filled the small space. Blue bedding, which seemed clean enough—I'd seen a lot worse over the years—covered the bed. I pressed my hand into the surface. Firm.

Nice mattress, that was always a plus. The matching blue curtains were partially drawn. Stepping forward, I pulled them back. The room must have held a corner location because the window hidden behind the curtains was a triangular shaped bay, jutting out at a point. The glass was leaded and dark, barely letting any light in. I tried the handle to see if I could lift the catch and see what laid beyond the dingy glass, but it didn't budge.

"It's... er." I couldn't think of any adjectives to describe the room.

"It sucks doesn't it? No one stays in this room longer than a few days. The last person who slept in this room swapped schools after three."

"Three days?" I cocked my head to the side. "Are you for real?"

Philomena grinned and swiped her hand across her chest. "Hope to die, truth."

I frowned. "What? Why would you hope to die?"

She laughed and perched on the bed. "Haven't you heard that before?"

"Uh, no." I shook my head. This conversation was getting weird, so I turned it to my normal firing of questions. I was happy asking questions—not so down with the answering them myself. "How long have you been here for, and exactly how many rules are there?"

She gazed at the ceiling. "Well, let me think. I'm seventeen now, so..." She counted on her fingers and I stared in horror as she reached her tenth digit. Peeling laughter, she waved her hand at me. "I'm kidding. I've been here a year. My parents are archaeologists; they found the school while they were up here on a dig."

"And?"

She shrugged. "And then they had to go on another dig,

called away unexpectedly. Some big find in Rome, apparently." She studied her fingernails. "Although what's left to find in Rome, I have no idea. That place has been pillaged and sold to the tourists." She lifted her face and gave me a small smile. "So here I am. It's not too bad." She glanced about the room and I watched her shiver and curl her shoulder in. She wasn't wrong. The room was chilled and damp. I was going to die of consumption in a decrepit Scottish castle. On the plus side, maybe a prince would come along and save me. "And, as for the rules, the staff think there are rules, but I can't think of a single one that's kept."

I nodded a little at this piece of good news. The only good news of the day. The uniform was one thing, attending lessons was another... if I had to follow a strict list of rules I had no hope of remembering with my scatter-brain approach to life, I couldn't see me lasting longer than one night in Fire Stone.

I don't know what I was thinking. Maybe it was jet lag, maybe it was the Scottish fresh air, but I blurted, "I'd love to be an archaeologist, it's always been my dream." The moment the words were out of my mouth I cringed.

I sounded like an idiot.

I'd never been able to explain the interest the earth held for me, all the secrets it contained. But, I didn't need to tell a complete stranger about them.

"Really? It always looked dull to me. But, I guess it pays well. Mum and Dad can afford to keep me here with the insane fees."

I sat on the bed, careful not to get too close. I didn't want to seem overfamiliar—or desperate. "It's not about money, or fame, although who doesn't dream of finding a unique world view changing artefact. It's kind of hard to explain." I shrugged.

"I can truthfully say I've never dreamed of that." She sniggered a little, but I let it pass. She had a fair point. Sobering her face, she waved for me to continue. "Please, tell me why you like it so much. Maybe I can get Mum and Dad to give you some holiday experience."

Perking up at the prospect of a connection to the world I longed to join, I tucked my feet up under my legs. Philomena was the most real person I'd met in a long time. There was nothing bubble-gum fake about her. I'd known her five minutes and she was already talking about introducing me to her mum and dad.

My cheeks blushed a warm burn. "I know it's geeky, and I don't go around telling everyone, but it's like the earth is talking to me. It wants to tell me things."

Silence swept around us. A drip from outside the window the only sound.

"Okay, make sure you only tell me things like that. The girls here, well, they are privately educated, a lot are snobs. Not to say they aren't fun, and they aren't all the same. But talking to them about the fact you want to roll in the earth and hear its voice... It's not going to go down well."

I scrunched my face. "That's not what I said." Why did I even say anything? What was I thinking? I knew better than that. I uncrossed my legs and started to shuffle towards the edge of the bed.

"Hey, hey. Don't go all G.I. Jane. It's cool." She grasped my hand in an unexpected act of familiarity. "I think we're going to be cool."

"Thanks." My cheeks flamed with chagrin.

"How's your time keeping though? Honestly, if I'm going to find a new bestie, then it's got to be someone who gets me to class on time."

"Bestie?" I shuddered a laugh. "Let's not get too carried away."

"Hey, you're my only American friend. It's destiny, plus, lemme guess, you want to meet a prince."

"Who? Me?"

"Don't all Americans want to come over here, drive around in a Volkswagen Beetle and accidentally knock over the heir to the throne and fall wildly in love?"

I paused. "Isn't that a movie?"

She shrugged. She was insane. Crazy. I liked her. "Well, I can introduce you to a prince. Come on. Did you want to get changed? Put some make-up on?" She went to grab for my duffle, her fingers on the zip.

"No, it's okay." I tried to block her. "It won't take me long." I glanced ruefully at my tiny bag containing my everything.

"Sure thing, New Yorker."

"How do you know I'm from New York?" Technically it was Queens, worlds apart, but I wasn't going to split hairs over it.

"Let's just say I'm a whizz with the computer."

"You had access to my file?" I cringed. Did she know I was an orphan? Did she know I'd spent ten years by myself?

"I'd use the word access very loosely. But, believe me, working in the school office to pay for some of my fees has its perks."

"You work in the office?"

"Sure I do. I said my mum and dad did well; I didn't say they were rolling rich." She fluffed out her wild halo of curls, leaning into a mirror with aged and darkened glass. Standing up, I stood next to her and peered at myself. I frowned at what I saw. Straight red hair and grey eyes peeked back at me. My mother had been a true redhead. It was one of my only memories of her; seeing her hair in the sunlight and thinking it looked like strands of fire. I had a watered down muted version: neither brown, nor red. "Believe me, it's better than working in the school kitchen, no one wants to smell of cabbage all day." She spun me around, her fingers on my elbow, and assessed me. Clearly approving of what she found, she gave me a reassuring smile.

"Come on, I'll give you a tour. Hopefully we will have missed all lessons by the time we've finished."

"That would be a plus."

"Come on then. Fire Stone first, and then we'll find your prince."

I took one last glance at myself in the mirror, pulling down the hem of my sweater so it sat straight on my hips.

"Sure, find me a prince." I laughed. As Philomena pulled me through the doorway back into the draughty hallway, I glanced back into room thirteen and could have sworn I saw a stirring in the shadows by the window. Ignoring the brush of wind and the chill on my nerves, I ploughed after Philomena. Whatever this tour contained, apparently it was at top speed.

"So this is the mess hall." She waved her arms at the cavernous space. Once it must have been the great hall of the castle. The vaulted ceiling above was scored with old worn beams, tired from holding up the weight of the roof for hundreds of years.

Philomena had given me a whirlwind run-down on the history of Fire Stone. The castle had been built on an ancient settlement, but no owners of the castle had ever stayed more than one generation before moving on to warmer, drier, more secure abodes. The school had been created a hundred years before, and it was the only institution to stand its ground within the ruins of the castle. The thick stone walls themselves dated back to the time of England's Edward I. He'd brought war and destruction to the borders of Scotland in his bid to claim the land and quell the Scottish chiefs. But he'd never penetrated Fire Stone, nor got close. Some said the land was cursed before he'd even got here.

"You know a lot about this," I'd said when Philomena had given me a lively battle recount.

She'd grimaced. "I know, it makes me sound like a real geek, but I'm not, I promise. It's just my parents were so obsessed with this land. I guess I just grew up knowing it all without really having to learn anything."

My heart panged at what it must be like to grow up with parents who talked to you, shared their excitement with you.

But I didn't need sentimentality. I didn't have time for it.

"Here, come on, let's get some food, I'm starved," she said, stopping my pity parade for one.

I cast a quick gaze over Philomena. She didn't look starved, but my stomach growled and I willingly allowed her to tow me along to a hot serving counter. Round lights glared down on what already looked like dried-up meat, cabbage, and potatoes. I smiled at the woman behind the counter. Her hair tied up under a cotton cook's hat, she was flushed and dabbing at her forehead with her arm. "I'm a vegetarian. Do you have anything?"

"Aye, lassie, I do."

Philomena snorted and elbowed me in the ribs as the

woman served up a plate toweringly high with extra cabbage and boiled potatoes.

"No lentils, or tofu? Protein maybe?"

She gave me another spoonful of cabbage. With a shudder at my plate and eternally grateful I wasn't sharing a dorm with a whole bunch of other gas-filled girls, I turned for the counter. I had a little cash in my pocket I could pay with. I'd changed a few spare dollars into not many pounds at the airport.

There was no counter. It was odd. We didn't have to pay for anything. No fingertip payment on a touchpad like I'd always known. We just took our towering plates of cabbage and walked to a table. Philomena guided us towards a table with six girls.

"Hey, this is Maeve." She nodded her head towards me, her hands busy attempting to get her plate onto the table without losing a potato.

"Mae," I corrected. I tried to smile at the people around the table, but my lips wouldn't behave and stretched into an odd shaped leer. With sweaty palms, I lowered my own tray before I dropped it and made a scene.

Six sets of eyes lifted to mine, and I gave an awkward wave.

"Mae's from America," Philomena announced, and I wanted to kick her feet under the table. I tried, but she was just out of reach. My foot connected instead with the shin of a blonde girl with elfin features and dazzling blue eyes.

"Ow." She bent down and rubbed her leg.

"Shit, I'm sorry. I didn't mean to—" I trailed off.

"Language." A sharp voice called across the room. I turned slightly and found Mrs Cox glaring at me. I gave a wave of apology before dropping my gaze to my lunch companions.

"Bloody hell, has she got bat hearing?" I muttered.

"Language!"

A giggle ran around the table. "Okay, so, introductions." Philomena continued her role as tour guide. Although as far as I could tell the tour so far had only included draughty hallways, dark and dim classrooms, and a wing we were forbidden to go in because it housed the male dorms.

I'd been almost relieved to see the odd male student walking about. I was beginning to think Fire Stone had its own unique segregation system.

"This is..." Philomena jumped into listing a bunch of names, jabbing her fingers at the girls around the table. "Blah, blah, blah, blah," was all I heard.

I chuckled, brushing at my hair as my cheeks warmed to an uncomfortable temperature. "Okay, I'll say sorry now because I won't remember who's who for a while."

I doubted very much I'd ever learn them. I didn't plan to stay—just long enough to say hi to my mysterious aunt and then I'd head down to London.

Philomena speared a greying potato with her fork. "Make yourself at home, Yankee, it's going to be a long afternoon."

I nudged the boiled cabbage around my plate. I'd heard the brits loved their stodgy food, but this was something else.

"What's up, Mae?"

I lifted my gaze to find a blonde-haired, slate-eyed girl watching me. The skin around her eyes bunched as she grinned. "Don't you like cabbage?"

I grimaced and stabbed a soggy strand with the tip of my fork. "I've been some places with an abstract view of cooking, but this is something else."

Not one to go hungry, I placed the limp leaf in my mouth and chewed. And then chewed and then chewed.

The girl with the blonde hair whose name I hadn't even registered, burst into a peal of laughter. "Oh my god, you should see your face."

I nodded, my lips clamped, and continued to chew. It was only a tiny piece of cabbage but it seemed to last forever. "So, tell us." She leant forward, her gaze quick, her hand darting in her hair and brushing at imaginary loose strands. "Why did you come all this way, to here of all places?" She took a bite of her chicken but continued to speak despite its obstruction. "Where are your parents? Is this some form of punishment? Are you a tearaway teenager intent on bringing music to your backwater town?"

I narrowed my eyes. "Isn't that a movie?"

Philomena snorted. "I've already tried that one, Charlie."

Charlie, *mental note taken,* poked her tongue at Philomena. I was just grateful she'd finished chewing her food.

"Well." I swallowed. All eyes were on me. I was an under-the-radar girl. My neck began to prickle with heat and sweat. "I don't come from a backwater. I've lived around Queens, New York, all my life." It was silly but my heart gave a little squeeze as I said the next words. "And my parents died when I was seven." I offered a shrug. I'd learned years before that the shrug at the end could stop the three-step awkward *shit your parents are dead* process. The shrug told them you were resigned to the news and dealing with it.

The table met my announcement and shrug with silence. A pale girl at the end, her hair the colour of ash bark, gave me a sympathetic smile. "Murder? Robbery gone wrong?"

Philomena rolled her eyes.

I cracked a smile. "Just a road accident—sorry to be dull."

The girl groaned, but Philomena shushed her. "Honestly, your fetish with death is starting to creep me out, Rach."

Grinning, the girl shrugged. "What can I say? I have diverse interests."

Unable to tell if this was a serious conversation or not, I studied my plate trying to work out how on earth I was going to survive in this place without starving to death. "Do we get to go to any local shops? I'm going to need to stock up on food."

Philomena shook her head. "No chance, it's too far. Occasionally we get taken into Braemar village. But it's just ad hoc, when they fancy taking the minibus out of the garage and ferrying us about."

I thought of the letter from my aunt, and the fact I stupidly didn't even know I was coming to a school. "Do you know a Mrs Melerion?" I asked.

All eyes swivelled to mine. "She's the school proprietor but she's never here, not ever. Every so often she sends gifts: random artefacts that get put into cabinets along the hallways, all ancient." Philomena studied me closely. "Why?"

"Because she's my aunt," I said before quickly adding, "Great aunt, and now legal guardian."

If I'd said I'd arrived from the moon there would have been less reaction. "Are you sure?" Charlie swept her hair in front of her face, an impromptu curtain. I glanced behind me to see what she was hiding from—nothing apart from children tackling cabbage.

"Well, she sent me a letter, that's why I'm here." I shrugged. "It seems if she's my legal guardian, what she says goes. It was delivered by an attorney, there was paperwork." I cringed.

When I said it out loud, it seemed preposterous I'd fly all this way because a man in a suit delivered me a letter from an unknown relative and waved a wad of paperwork at me which said I'd upped my family members by a whole one hundred per cent. But then, what did I have to stay in the states for?

"And she put you in room thirteen?" Philomena tipped her head to the side. "I'm guessing family feud."

"I don't know. I'd never heard of her. Because my parents died when I was so young, I guess I never got to ask them things which may have become important at a later date." I was being facetious, but I was uncomfortable and squirming. Mainly for not exploring more about my aunt before I left the states. And I was the girl with all the questions. What a fail.

Philomena grinned at me. "I think I can feel a budding friendship growing here."

I couldn't help but smile back. "Maybe, if you stop asking daft questions."

She shook head. "That could be a deal breaker. I'm full of stupid questions."

"Me too." A bustle by the entrance to the grand hall pulled my attention.

"Ha-ha!" Philomena sounded pleased. "Now, you owe me, but I told you I was going to introduce you to a Prince."

I glared at her. "What are you talking about?"

"Prince!" She hollered. "Over here."

Tilting her head towards my shoulder she whispered, "Tristan Prince, twelve o'clock." I followed her gaze and watched the man staring back at us. I say man. He was big: powerfully built—not your average teenage boy. But in the open planes of his face was a youthful glow, wide lips, and deep dark eyes.

A terrible pounding stomped across my chest. I clutched a hand over my mouth, sure I was going to be sick. His onyx gaze bore into the space I filled, his eyes narrowing, the tendons in his neck standing out as he clenched his hands into fists at his side. He looked like he wanted to kill me.

And that was okay.

Because I wanted to kill him.

I strained in my seat. My legs, my arms, they all wanted me across the room with my hands across his throat.

"Mae, what's wrong? You look like you've seen a ghost."

I struggled to face Charlie. Her hand crept cross the table, soothing and calm, but I snatched my own away. Philomena held onto my elbow while I vibrated with rage.

"I've got to go." I almost shouted the words. The whole time I tried to raise myself up, all I could think was it would be immensely satisfying to sink a sharp blade into that wide chest.

Tristan Prince watched me rise from my seat, his face etched into a bitter scowl. Using all my strength, I fled past him out into the dark hallway without landing a punch on his jaw.

Somehow, I ran back to room thirteen, following the endless corridors and low ceilings. I burst through the door and landed on the bed.

What was that? I rolled and stared at the ceiling. His dark, furious gaze was burned into my memory. I'd wanted to kill him. To thrust my hand into his chest and rip out his heart.

I must be tired? Must have jet lag?

Either that, or I was allergic to Scotland. Maybe it was a

severe reaction to the cabbage? What was his excuse though? Other than being an American-hating lunatic perhaps? I didn't know. I'd expected the day to be awkward, uncomfortable, and ever so slightly exciting. After all this was my first trip abroad. My first trip anywhere. Then, Tristan Prince had ruined it all with that burning coal gaze and my need to remove his face with my fingernails. That wasn't in my daily plan at all.

It was as if we were born to hate one another—it was deep within me. How many random guys had I glanced over during the last seventeen years? I'd never wanted to murder one before. I'd never wanted to murder anyone.

I closed my eyes, still seeing his hate-filled gaze. I shuddered and hoped sleep would find me. A chilled breeze slipped into the room and I attempted to free the blanket from under my back to wrap across my chest. The sounds of birds chirping in distant trees lulled me like white noise. Somewhere water ran free and fast. I'd have to ask Philomena tomorrow where the river was...

3

Caledonia

"**M**ae!" A screech caught my attention, and I glanced up to find my sister running across the camp. She was grinning, her face flushed, but it didn't stop me jumping to my feet. Alana was the epitome of decorum. So, even her breaking into a fast walk told me something was amiss. A run meant something monumental was occurring.

"What say you, Alana?" I smiled my greeting.

"Agnese is having her baby." Alana screeched to a halt, flying dust in front of me. I dropped my needlework; it was terrible anyway. I'd only been using it as a distraction from my true job in hand: memorising endless law and scripture. Over and over again I had to silently repeat it. Poking a needle through cotton as a form of distraction seemed to help.

"That's fantastic." I smiled, but then noticed the tightening of skin around Alana's eyes. "What's wrong?"

"The baby. It's not the right way up. It's been in the same position for a while."

"Why are you here?" I grabbed her by the arm, spinning her with considerable force, "Get Heather, she will help."

Alana fought back against my firm push. "You don't understand, Mae. It was Heather who asked for you."

"I know nothing about birthing bairns, and I am certainly no Kneel Woman." I was years away from learning how to coax a new life into the world: bairn, lamb, even pup. And I was glad.

Alana paused, her eyes searching my face. "Heather thinks you do. Come, Mae, please. They are both going to die."

I grabbed at the cotton dress which hung around my ankles and hoisted it up, flinging back my red robe of learning. Free of the tangle of material around my feet, I was able to make to Agnese's hut in record time. Alana lagged behind. I may not know anything about childbirth, but I wasn't about to let that stop me from helping a member of our tribe. Small and close, every member of our settlement was family to me.

Agnese's screams split the air and I shuddered impulsively, gulping a breath of cool freshness into my lungs as I pushed through the wooden door. A couple of other village women stood by the doorway, wringing their hands. I nodded to them as I swept in. Heather was stooped over the pale generous legs of Agnese. A rancid smell filled the air. I glanced at the bed to find it covered in a nasty green liquid. It looked as if I'd spilled a bowl of herbs soaked in water. I stepped up, holding my breath from the smell of sweat and foul liquid, and touched Heather on the arm. Her tense face relaxed when she saw me, and she pulled me to one side.

Another of the village women stepped forward to take her place, mopping Agnese's brow with dampened linen.

"Thank goodness you're here, My Lady. This goes very ill indeed." She muttered silently under her breath and raised her eyes to the roof of the round house. "May the goddess help us in our time of need."

I held her arm. Her face was flushed, her chest rising and falling, sweat across her brow. In fact, she didn't look that different to the poor woman on the bed giving birth. "Heather, I don't know what I can do. My training is incomplete. I know nothing of this."

Heather stopped panting, her breath becoming calm. She raised her hands and cupped my face in the most motherly of holds. "I believe you know how to help. Will you try?"

Her words meant little. I didn't know what I didn't know and according to Druid lore and training, I knew very little. But, as I glanced at the woman on the bed, she was fading, her colour dipping. The child inside her would be worse.

"Come," I said. "Tell me what you want me to do." Swallowing my fear, I stepped for the bed, smoothing my hand across the feverish skin of Agnese. "Agnese, can you hear me?" I leant down and spoke in the woman's ear, but she didn't acknowledge me. The labour of birth had her in its grip.

I placed my palm on her forehead and breathed deeply. It seemed natural and foreign all at once. My eyes closed and I focused. I had no knowledge to reach for but that in my head. I rotated through everything I'd learned so far: every cycle, every harvest, every boon we prayed for. A deep calm settled within me.

When I opened my eyes, Agnese's skin seemed a hint less sallow.

Heather was watching me, her gaze sharp. "The baby hasn't turned. He's upside down and facing the wrong way."

Unable to help myself, I winced, squeezing my legs together. Childbirth may be a natural gift, but it looked like it could rip you inside out. There was nothing natural about that, surely? I focused, pushing away my own abhorrence and focused myself on harvest and boon, all the things we needed, all the benefits and rewards we earned. Life was one of those. A warm flow, like the glow of liquid metal spreading through my limbs.

"What should I do to help?"

Heather moved quickly, snatching my hand from where it was placed on Agnese's forehead, lowering them to her swollen belly. "Next time she cries, hold the baby, feel the baby, and will it to move."

I glanced up at her set face in confusion. "I can't will it to move."

She frowned. "Fine, My Lady. Lay your hands on it, that's all."

Agnese began to pant, her head shaking from one side to the other as she groaned and muttered various words I was sure she'd regret when of her own mind again. I raised my hand back to her head trying to soothe her.

"Not her! The baby!" Heather made me jump, but I settled my hands back over the baby. The stretched skin of Agnese's tummy was shiny and smooth. Blocking distracting thoughts, I searched out that golden liquid glow, finding it hidden, waiting within my veins. When Agnes screamed I concentrated on the gold, willing it to travel to my palms.

Agnese reared off the bed. The village woman, whose face I couldn't see—so focused as we were on Agnese—stepped up and mopped her brow.

"Good," Heather cried. Ducking her head between

Agnese legs, she assessed the situation. "Come on, Aggie, another nice big push."

The poor woman covered in sweat cried, her lips trembling. "No, I can't."

Heather wasn't having that. "Of course you can; even My Lady is here to help. You must push."

Agnese's eyes flew open and a burn carried up my cheeks. "Don't worry about anything, Aggie. Let's get this baby born." I tried to soothe her, the whole time watching Heather take up position as if she were attempting to catch a flaming arrow.

She began to pant again. I soothed my hands, crooning to the bump. Under the skin, a kick met my hands. "That's fine, little one. You wiggle around, you have plenty of room."

Astounded, I watched as a ripple shifted under the stretched parchment of Agnese's tummy, rolling under my hands with a firm push.

"That's it," Heather cried. "That's it, two more pushes."

Agnese wasn't thrilled at this news, another broad oath making its way to our ears. But the baby had a mind its own. Three screams, pushes, and vivid words later, and he squirmed his way into Heather's outstretched hands.

My eyes filled with tears. Purple, and yelling for attention, the little scrap didn't look like it should have caused as much pain as it had.

Agnese began to pale, her skin sheening with sweat. Heather glanced up and frowned. "My Lady, if you wouldn't mind." She nodded at Agnese and instinctively I stepped forward, smoothing my hands around her face once more. I whispered, but what I muttered I didn't know. It was nothing my father had taught me. When Agnese opened her eyes, and met my gaze, I breathed a thankful sigh of relief. "Your son, My Lady." I dropped the brave woman a curtsey as Heather stepped up with the hollering and distraught newborn.

Agnese clutched him to her breast and he suckled, rooting for her bosom. Slowly, I slipped away, edging backwards out of the door.

"Thank you, My Lady." Heather's eyes met mine, cool and direct.

"I was merely a bystander to your skill." I bobbed her a curtsey and the old woman flushed, pushing at her wet hair with an arm. She gave me a smile, but I sensed in her glance I'd be having a conversation with her before long.

Outside the air was cool and refreshing, and the crisp evening chill refreshed my lungs.

"My Lady." I started at the voice behind me, but when a playful hand snaked around my waist I relaxed.

"Tristram, you shocked the life out of me."

I turned to face the younger son of our lord and chief. "Any excuse to be close to you." His eyes burned, and I dipped my gaze.

"Tristram!" The deep timbre, familiar to everyone living in the settlement, boomed through the chilling air. Tristram's gaze held my own before a lightning quick smile flashed across his face.

"Father." He held his hands wide as he opened his arms in greeting. I cast my own gaze towards Alen, our chief, not surprised to see him flanked by his high priest in his flowing white robes. Making eye contact with the spiritual leader of our clan, I made my way towards them, one step behind Tristram. As much as he was flamboyant in his greeting, daring and bold with his bow of respect, I was meek and reserved.

"Mae, what brings you away from your studies?"

I lifted my face to meet the gaze of the white-robed man. "Agnese had her baby, Father. I was called on to assist."

His stare remained on my face for an elongated pause until Alen shouted, "The bonny babe has arrived." The chief nudged me with an elbow. A giant of a man, standing nearly as tall and as wide as a tree, he almost sent me flying. I ignored the smirking twitch of Tristram's lips and looked at his father. "A boy, My Lord, and a bonny one too, and loud."

My own father's eyes bore down. He'd want details later, starting with why I'd been called. What could I say? Heather insisted?

"This deserves a feast." Alen turned to the loose circle shape of the settlement. "A feast in honour of our newest member." A couple of children gave a shout and whoop, scampering off towards their parents.

Father frowned, but Alen turned to him with a wide, golden smile. "So serious, my priest, always so serious."

Father edged him away but I could still hear his words. "And what do you plan to feast on? We have no meat and little stores."

Alen patted him on his back not to be deterred. "Did you hear that, Tristram? Our high priest wants to know what we shall feast on."

Tristram stepped forward his face glowing. "I'm happy to oblige."

"Take your men and make a kill to feed us all."

My stomach lurched and I glanced warily at Tristram's excited expression. I wanted to hold him back, but I couldn't.

He strode off to gather hunting men, and I chased after him, skipping to the side so my objective wasn't obvious. "You plan to be skewed by a wild boar, My Lord?"

Tristram's eyes lit with mirth, a glittering depth to his jet orbs. "You do care!" He flourished me a low bow, his voice too loud to be a private conversation. Folding my arms across my chest, I watched his little display.

"I care for the wellbeing of our leaders, as is my job and position." His lips curved at the edges and he stepped forward, his body aligning with mine like stars in the sky. I shifted. "You play games, Tristram. Are you ever serious?" His eyes swept along me.

"Sometimes."

"You've been like this since we were children, but soon we will have to grow up and take our place within the settlement."

His face flickered with a darkened cloud. "I know my place, Mae. I am the merry brother of those in power, expected to please and court our people. What is your role?"

My cheeks flamed. "You know my role, Tristram. Don't tease so. I shall train to be a priestess and then I will be of real service to our people." I was harsh.

"Well, I am fulfilling the role my father carved for me, I shall be satisfied with that."

"Really?" Unwittingly, I stepped closer. The man in front of me was a powerful, impressive echo of the boy I'd grown up alongside. "You are happy playing the merry prince?"

His eyes dropped to my mouth, "I could be happier with you by my side. Maybe you are the push I need to grow up?" His words were a low rumbled echo and my stomach twisted. As close as he was, the golden skin along his neck rising from the collar of his tunic willed me to reach out and touch it. His eyes, when he looked deep within mine, held an unexpected solemnity in their depths.

"That's for our fathers to decide." I trembled with the words, my body heating. I could deny the connection between Tristram and I on the outside. But, inside, deep within the secrets of my heart, I knew there would never be

another I'd want. There would never be another I'd entertain
the prospect of.

He stepped back, the spell weaving between us urging us
closer, broken. "Would you care to come on the hunt, My
Lady? You could be there to assist when I get skewered." I
watched as his confident mask slipped back into place. He
made his voice louder. "Mae is coming on the hunt. Which
other maidens wish to partake? We will make it a party."

Frowning, I slipped away. This Tristram I had no time
for—the jester, the entertainer. An ache settled in my chest
and I knew what it was. Remorse for the man I knew he
could be.

I did attend the hunt. But I kept towards the back, my eyes
sweeping for danger. The wild forest loomed overhead, its
dark shadows stretching with every passing moment. "It's
getting late." I turned to Alana at my side. Her hand slipped
into mine.

"We should turn back, the festival for Agnese will have
to be delayed."

I tutted. "You know Tristram. He will never return
empty handed."

"You talk to him, he listens to you. We've circled the
settlement three times with no sign of a quarry."

Alana was different to me. She was pale and regal, her
actions smooth and restrained. I was the opposite. She was
the moon to my earth. As two sisters, we couldn't be more
different. I loved her, though, even when she did give way to
unnecessary worry.

Linking my hand through her arm, I anchored us tight
together knowing she would benefit from the security. Dusk
was stretching into night and what had been a chilled breeze

was now a stiff cold wind. I longed to be back by the fire, toasting my hands and listening to the lore as my father fulfilled his role of bard and entertained our people with feats of the past. It wasn't his only role, but it was the one he maintained that I enjoyed the most. "Do you worry about Father?" I asked the question low.

"Shh." I wasn't low enough for Alana's liking. "What do you mean? Keep it down, Mae. There are ears everywhere and not everyone agrees with Father's ways." I glanced at her in the darkening light.

"You talk of the rumours of the newcomers, the invaders who have settled south of our borders?"

"I heard father and Alen talking," she whispered into my ear. I leant towards her, keeping one eye on Tristram leading the march at the front. "He says the southern lands are taken. The newcomers, they are building a new settlement, greater than anything anyone has ever seen."

I wanted to close my eyes to dream of what this settlement could look like. I locked the thought away for when we were safely home and weren't walking in the dark.

"Hard times are coming, I think," I whispered.

Her glance when she met mine was pale and ethereal. "They are already here, Mae. Have you not been to the store and seen the supplies? We won't survive the winter."

"We will." I gritted my teeth with such ferocity I made my head pound. "We must. Our people won't be defeated by invaders or hunger."

She smiled, a small wan upturn of her lips. "I hope you are right, sister. Now, please." Her smile widened further. "Please go speak to Tristram, he listens to you. We shall go back empty handed, this is futile." She shivered. "And I'm cold."

I stared at Tristram's broad back. His smooth muscles

shifted, and he clutched his spear. My mouth dried and I swallowed hard. "Okay, but you know he hates to be defeated."

Alana mumbled under her breath, but I didn't catch her words as I stepped up calling Tristram's name. I was closing in to his position when a loud shout rose. "Deer!"

He was gone, chasing into the woods without a backwards glance. I shivered, my insides churning. Last time someone had gone chasing after a deer they'd been found with their guts on the wrong side of their body, their soul cycled back into the fabric of time.

"Tristram," I rose my voice in panic, and picked up my skirts. "Curse it." I leapt after him into the dark foliage. He wasn't going to lose his guts to a boar if I had anything to do with it.

I was too late.

The deer was already slung over Declan—Tristram's man at arms—shoulders. Its glassy eyes berating me for not giving it an escape route. We're hungry, I thought. And pretty as you are, you'll taste good.

Tristram panted as he came up to me. "Did I have you worried, My Lady?" I frowned and turned my gaze away from his red tipped spear.

"Only that you may trip and fall in the dark and we'd have to haul you back home."

He grinned, his arm snaking over my shoulders and he tucked me. A light pressure landed on my hair. I stiffened. Did he just kiss my head? A burning blush crept along my skin. "You may pretend not to care, Mae. But I know otherwise."

I glowed under his touch but slunk out from under it. "Come, we have a hungry village to feed."

"Aye, we do." He picked up his pace and I followed behind.

Alana skipped up to my side, her footsteps lighter now she knew we were on the homeward march. "You shall be married by the time of Mabon." She cast me a pointed glance, and my cheeks warmed a little.

I watched Tristram pull his horn from his belt. The sound of the bellow startled birds from the trees. Muscled and powerful, he was beautiful. A gift from the god's.

I wished I could believe what she said was true. But in my heart, I didn't feel it.

"I don't think so."

My path wasn't clear to me. I wished it was. I wished I had the sight my father contained as bard. I wished I knew what the future held for all of us.

We were walking back into the settlement, our arrival greeted with cheers. Men had optimistically started a huge fire, and women were waiting to prepare the kill, when I remembered I hadn't spoken to Alana about father's strange behaviour. It was too late now, too many ears were around.

A prickle darted over my skin and I glanced around finding the narrowed eyes of my father settled on me.

Tristram blasted his horn again and the whole settlement: man, woman, and child, gave a giant cheer. This would be a feast—but how long the good fortune would last... I couldn't be sure.

4

A loud bellow made me jump, and I sat up, fighting against the tangled sheets. My eyes stung with sleep and I rubbed at them. What was that noise? Through blurry vision, I glanced around the room, finding my meagre belongings still in their duffle where I'd left them in room thirteen. It was freezing, and shivering compulsively, I wrapped the blanket around my shoulders and gingerly put my feet on the cold stone floor. The window was wide open. Fresh blasting air and drizzly rain swept into the bedroom, turning the curtains into billows of blue cotton. No wonder I was cold. I shut it with a slam checking the latch. Frowning, I gave it a hard wiggle. Didn't I struggle to open that yesterday? Another shiver made the hairs on my arms stand on end. I grabbed at my duffel and pulled out a Yankees hoodie, tugging it over my head and pulling the sleeves down over my hands. It still smelled faintly of aftershave and I breathed in deeply. The scent was a snapshot of the past—a could have been moment—which had turned to never being anything; the jersey the only reminder of a short-lived romance.

When the letter from my aunt arrived, it seemed the perfect opportunity to break off something that wasn't going anywhere. Still, the hoodie was a bonus.

I glanced around the stone walls. Even with the window shut the curtains still moved with a slight sway. This place was creepy. Why would people pay to send their children here? In the middle of nowhere, damp, cold, and lacking in all comforts. It didn't make any sense to me.

A yawn made me stretch. I'd been sound asleep until the wind and rain had woken me. I scrubbed a hand down my face. I felt dirty, travel tired, and all out exhausted. What I needed was a hot shower and some kick-ass coffee of the nuclear variety.

"Are you ready?" A loud bang landed on the door, shaking it on its hinges. Scurrying over the cold floor, I opened the door to find Philomena slouching on the other side against the doorframe, munching on an apple in her hand. If possible, her hair was wilder, the curls having multiplied as if she'd been out in the rain for a morning run. I wasn't one to judge, but she didn't seem the jogging type.

"Philomena?" I groaned and slumped my shoulders. "It's so early, what are you doing?"

"Please call me Phil, I can't stand Philomena." Her face scrunched with distaste. "It makes me think of my gran, and those awful teas I used to have to sit through around her kitchen table. She'd tell us stories of the war."

I smiled and opened the door wider for her to slip through. "Sounds kind of nice." The thought of sitting around a kitchen table participating in friendly banter wasn't an alien concept to me. Not all my homes over the years had been devoid of childhood cornerstones. However, they had been few and far between. The older I got, the more I'd been left to my own devices. The care system at the age of seventeen largely became a roof over your head and a half-stocked fridge.

As if she could read my mind she shook her head. "Don't think it was all some rose-tinted moment of family bonding. She repeated the same story every time we went."

"Maybe she was muddled."

Phil snorted. "Or batshit crazy. I asked mum once why she always told the same tale. Apparently, she was born at the end of the war. She didn't even see any of it." She chuckled. "I believed her for years."

She sat on my bed and watched me expectantly through thick black-rimmed glasses. It took me a moment to work out why she looked so different. "Did you have glasses on yesterday?" I asked.

"Nah." She frowned and shook her curls. "I hate contact lenses. So, I try them and then remember I hate them. Tomorrow I shall try them again."

I chuckled and searched out my wash bag from my duffel. Philomena had pointed out the bathroom on my tour the previous day. I wasn't unused to sharing bathrooms with near strangers. What I wasn't excited about was the dash in the cold to get to it. "Are you going to sit here while I wash-up?" I asked. It was oddly comforting. Phil and I seemed to have clicked so quickly. It didn't seem odd to leave her in my room while I left to use the bathroom.

She looked at me expectantly and glanced around the room. My lips twitched as she lifted the duvet and peered underneath. "What are you washing up? Have you been having a midnight feast without inviting anyone?"

We stared at one another for a long pause before I gave up with a sigh and shrugged my shoulders helplessly. "I don't know what you're talking about."

"Washing up? It's what one does to the dishes after eating?"

I took a moment to process and then it made sense. "Okay. Uh, no. I'm going to go and wash myself." I sniggered, and my cold nose dripped. I was definitely going to end up dying in this place, malnourished and freezing. "Is that better?" I grinned and wiped my nose with my towel.

She nodded, satisfied, and with a smile I slipped out the room. I was right, it was freezing. I shivered the whole way there, the whole time I was in the shower, and the whole way back again. By the time I closed my bedroom door and found Philomena flicking through my stuff, my teeth were chattering. "What are you doing?" was more of a "wha-wha-wha- oin." Which was all my teeth would allow.

"Unpacking for you. Seriously, Mae, you need to become more proactive."

I grimaced and picked up the uniform hanging on the outside of the cupboard, eyeing it with intense displeasure. "I've been asleep. I've only just woken up."

"You've been asleep the whole time, since yesterday lunch? Wow, no wonder your skin is so good, if you're getting sixteen hours of sleep a night."

I turned for the mirror. My skin wasn't that good. Pale and translucent, I'd rather have owned her earthy colouring, than my own. I dropped my towel onto the floor. My underwear was already in place after I'd squeezed into it while soaking wet and freezing in the bathroom, and then pulled the shirt over my shoulders. One thing I could be grateful for was that it seemed to fit. How my aunt had known what size to order was a mystery.

I yawned as I zipped up the skirt.

"How can you be yawning?" she asked.

"I don't know." I yawned again around my words. "But I'm so tired. I don't feel rested at all." I glanced in the mirror as I tucked my shirt in. "Maybe it's jet lag?" I'd never flown out of time zones before so had no idea what jet lag was supposed to feel like. If it meant feeling like death and like I wanted to crawl into a hole and never surface again—I had it.

"You need to get a wiggle on. We will miss breakfast, and I know how much you're going to love a nice hearty bowl of porridge."

I pulled a face which made her laugh. "Cabbage and porridge, this place is a delight for the taste buds."

"I know, and you haven't even met the teachers yet."

"Will we be in class together?" I asked with some optimism, not overly excited at walking around the creepy school by myself. I had no doubt that Phil would have checked my schedule if she'd have wanted. The classes were of no interest to me, I wasn't planning on staying anyway, but I'd always been conscientious in my studies. I guess it was a hard habit to break. It wouldn't be hard to humour this for a while as I waited for my aunt to come back and free me up to go and discover the rest of the country.

"Afraid not, Yankee. You've got double English this morning. Word of warning." She wiggled her dark, full eyebrows. "Hit the coffee hard, you're gonna need it."

"Thanks." I laughed and pulled on the blazer. I'd say a strait jacket would have more breathing space. "This is really uncomfortable. Do I have to wear it?" I couldn't remember the last time I'd tried to force myself into something so stiff and unyielding.

She nodded. "Yep, unless you want to have a love-in with Mrs Cox during detention this afternoon. Which you will if you break the uniform rules." She sighed. "Don't get me wrong, I'm all for independence and individuality; it's just really, there is nothing worse than a detention with Cox."

"I'll take your word for it and wear the damn thing." I grimaced though. It all felt suffocating and unnatural.

"Thought you would." She winked and got up from the bed, placing the pile of clothes she'd folded into a drawer. "Is this everything?"

I glanced at the pile. It was very small. "Yeah, I didn't have much to bring."

"Good thing you've uniform then."

"Thought we didn't get to go anywhere anyway?" Whilst it might be nice to put on a pair of jeans and get out of this weird damp castle, there hadn't looked like a lot of places to go on the drive here from the airport.

"True. Very, very true. But at the weekends we have to go outside for exercise and fresh air." She used her fingers to quote mark her words. "Lots of tramping about getting muddy."

I stared at her, shocked. "I don't do mud, I'm a city girl."

She grinned and walked for the door. "Not anymore. Don't worry, I've got some spare boots you can use."

"Thanks." I sent her a withering look. First a uniform and then tramping about in mud? This place couldn't get much worse.

But I was wrong.

Because there was English and then there was *him*. And that was a whole lot worse.

. . .

D uring my deep dreamless sleep, I'd forgotten about the strange events at lunch with the tall blond boy. Or would I say man? I still wasn't sure.

And neither would I be. Because I couldn't be in the room without wanting to kill him.

I pushed through the door to English. It gave a creak, but I was becoming used to the eerie sound effects. None of the hinges seemed to have been greased in the last hundred years or so. That wasn't the only sound effect to my arrival in English. My stomach gurgled and groaned, clenching with annoyance at my one meagre spoonful of porridge. Who puts salt in porridge? Nobody in their right mind, apart from the cooks at Fire Stone. I'd swallowed one spoonful and washed it down with weak coffee. I'd made Phil promise to divulge where she'd got the toast I'd seen her with when I'd arrived.

"Hi," I waved uncomfortably as I slipped in through the noisy door. Internally I cursed my great aunt and the fact she'd tracked me down and brought me all this way. The teacher was already up front stood by a blackboard wiping it clean with a cloth. She turned, and I gave her an apologetic smile. "Sorry I'm late, I got lost." Lost was an understatement. I'd walked for at least five minutes down the wrong corridor which didn't seem to lead anywhere. I needed a map, but I'd been assured at breakfast that such a luxury didn't exist.

"Maeve Adams, if I'm correct?" Another petite member of staff, but whereas Mrs Cox was tiny and birdlike, the English teacher was as short as she was wide. Her hair was piled in a greying dark bun on top of her head, a pencil poking through securing it in place, and it appeared no one had told her she had a splatter of breakfast down her fuzzy cardigan—or if they had, she didn't care.

"I prefer Mae." I stepped further into the room glancing about. The room was large and airy, almost warm, although where the heat was coming from in this rundown building I didn't know. It certainly wasn't outside where it was raining and had been constantly since breakfast. The sun didn't appear to exist in Scotland. If it did, it was on holiday.

"Mae, perfect." She concentrated hard, straining almost. "Right, I think I've remembered that. I'm Miss Barlow."

"Okay then..." I trailed off, unsure of what to say. I wasn't going to pull a funny face and pretend to try to remember her name.

There were a handful of chuckles, but I didn't lift my eyes. Last thing I needed was a laughing fit in my first class.

"Is this your first time to Scotland? I understand you come from the States." she asked.

I internalised my groan. *Please don't make me do the new kid speech.*

"First time," I mumbled, shuffling from foot to foot and staring at the flagstone floor.

"You will love it here, so much history, so many stories. It's a wealth of knowledge for the soul."

Another giggle lifted from the back of the classroom. I dared a peek from under my bangs and saw one of my companions from lunch yesterday sitting there grinning. She gave me a cheery wave and a thumbs up which Miss Barlow didn't catch. My eyes swept straight back to the floor. I mustn't laugh.

Barlow wasn't going to let me go without my saying something, so I mumbled about the rain, and that it seemed pretty from under cloud cover, but how I had jet lag... *please let me sit down now.*

She waved me off, and I marched breathing a sigh of relief, eyes down, to the back of the classroom. The desks were single wooden squares, scored with graffiti and compass puncture marks. I pulled on a metal chair when I found a desk empty near the girl from lunch. She gave me another wave, and I sent a small one back. Other eyes turned and landed on my spot at the back. It was hard to make out any distinguishing features when we were all wearing the same clothes. A few people nodded, and I smiled back, but really, I just wanted to hide out of view. It was like the first day at Kindergarten all over again. Everyone wanted to see the new girl. I didn't have many early memories but standing in the front of that classroom is one I've never forgotten; the swish of my mother's skirt as she'd pushed me gently forward with the palm of her hand.

There was no gentle maternal encouragement now. There hadn't been for a long time.

"We are reading Romeo and Juliet, Mae, have you studied it before?" Mrs Barlow said loudly, her voice almost lifting into song. She turned to me from the blackboard and I shrunk further into my seat. This time *everyone* looked at me, even the people who hadn't bothered before.

"Uh, yeah, a couple of times."

"And?" She clasped her hands together, tilted her head to the side and waited expectantly.

Did she want me to summarise my findings on the four-hundred-year-old play? I shifted uncomfortably, the neckline of my white, crisp, shirt sticking to my skin. Taking a deep breath, I told myself I could do this. I knew Romeo and Juliet, I'd studied it enough to be able to make a concise and authoritative assessment. "I think it's a tragic tale of stupidity."

The blonde from lunch snorted.

"Stupidity?" Mrs Barlow clasped her hands to her chest like I'd mortally wounded her with a flying arrow of burning words. She waddled down the aisle of desks to get closer to me.

My cheeks heated, and I coughed to clear my throat. What I really wanted to do was to grab a sheet of paper off the nearest desk and fan myself down. Hold on! My opinion was equally valid. Romeo and Juliet would be far more enjoyable as a play if they hadn't died at the end. "Well, yeah, I mean if the characters had just talked, expressed themselves, then half of the tragedies wouldn't have happened."

Barlow's mouth flapped open. "But without the tragedies how would the two families have united, which as the prologue tells us is the point of the play?" She perched a generous hip on my desk and it wobbled. I placed my feet on the bar underneath trying to anchor my desk in place.

I was thinking of a suitable counterargument when the door banged, and all eyes spun from Barlow and I to the front of the room.

There he was. Largely forgotten from my memories of yesterday. I stiffened. He filled the doorway, his shirt untucked, his tie askew. Bronzed and golden like a Roman statue, he seemed to bring the light of the sunshine with him. His hair was close-cropped, his lips wide and soft, his glare as black as the depth of night.

"Ah, Mr Prince, you are late, as usual." She beckoned him with the crook of her finger. "But you are missing a lively interpretation of our class text by Mae Adams here."

His dark and midnight eyes fell to where I hid behind

my desk. My fingers gripped the wood, holding myself from flying at him and gouging his eyes out. I could visualise it in goofy detail. I'd pierce his flesh with my fingers, lifting those coal eyes straight from their sockets. *What the hell?* A wave of nausea rocked me and sweat sprang along my forehead. *That's disgusting. What am I even thinking?*

His hands bunched into tight fists, the knuckles straining against his skin. His eyes burned with the fury of hell, while tendons strained in his neck. Under the golden tone of his skin he paled until he looked about as nauseous as I was feeling. He coiled, like a tiger about to pounce, but at the last moment he turned on his heel and slammed back out of the classroom.

An awkward silence filled the space. The air chilled, the unexpected warmth disappearing in the rush of wind from the slammed door. Mrs Barlow chuckled with force. "Tristan obviously isn't in the mood for Shakespeare this morning." She slipped from my desk, our conversation regarding my opinion thankfully forgotten. Fiddling on her desk she scrawled a note and then gestured a boy called Ben to the front of the classroom. "Take this to Mrs Cox please." She handed him the paper and waved him away.

She started to talk while sweeping loopy handwriting over the chalkboard. My skin crawled at the noise of the chalk scraping across the surface but that wasn't what was making me sick to my stomach.

As soon as Tristan Prince had left the room, I'd lost all desire to wear his eyeballs as a necklace. I went back to thinking about Romeo and Juliet and how stupid they were, but in the back of my mind the vision of Tristan's black burning eyes branded themselves into my memory. I gave a shiver and pulled my blazer tight across my middle.

. . .

The great hall was busier than lunch the day before. I'd survived the rest of the day without wanting to maim anyone. I'd had science with Phil which had turned dangerous when we'd miscalculated an experiment, and History with Charlie. By far, History was the best lesson. Mr Bonner, a muddled old man, hunched at the top of the spine, had kept me gripped. He'd made me want to go out and dig stuff up, and it had been a while since I'd felt that. A year to be precise. A year since I'd found out I would never be able to afford to go to college.

The lesson had only been marred by the fact I found myself watching the door, waiting to see if Tristan Prince would arrive and if he did what part of him I'd want to cut off next. I'd also spent a lot of time wondering why I wanted to chop him into small pieces and hide him in a freezer.

My eyes swept the dinner hall. He wasn't there, and my stomach dipped—with relief. "I hear English was exciting this morning?" Phil stabbed at some peas with her fork, they darted across her plate in escape.

"The teacher grilled me on Romeo and Juliet, it was awful. I don't think she liked my assessment."

Phil laughed. "I don't doubt it, she's obsessed with that play. We all study it every year no matter how many times we've done it before."

"Really" I scrunched my face. "I can't think why anyone would want to read it that much.

"Anyway, Miss-Diversion-Tactics, that's not what I'm talking about. Apparently, Tristan Prince stormed out when he saw you."

I flushed. "That's not true. It couldn't have been me, I've never spoken to him." This wasn't true. I didn't know what was going on, or even why, but I knew one very simple fact; I'd never hated anyone as much as I hated him. Irrational, insane, but true.

"Maybe." She shrugged pulling my attention back to our conversation. "I wonder what his problem is? Yes, he's an obnoxious, pretentious arse, but taking a disliking to you before you've properly met is rude even for him."

I didn't know whether to be relieved he was always standoffish, or to despair that he hated me on sight. But then what did that matter? The burn of fury I'd felt when I'd laid eyes on him still smouldered in my veins.

I wanted to chase him down and sock him in the face. But why? I couldn't even pretend that was a normal reaction.

I assessed my plate and couldn't find a single item I wanted to put in my mouth. "So," I tried to sound natural, "he's always moody like that?" I couldn't say his name, scared it was going to burn my throat with vile acid.

Her hazel eyes settled on my face and she pulled a face, her mouth full of peas. "Well you know, rich bitch, my dick's gonna itch."

I snorted, a bubble of laughter making me cough until I was close to suffocating. I placed my head on the table and tried to stay alive. This castle was going to kill me with starvation and damp, not by giggling. "So, he sleeps around?" I wasn't surprised. He looked like girls would drag themselves limbless to lie in his path.

She shrugged, the tips of her ears tingeing pink. "Not in this direction." She stabbed at her plate again. "Anywhooo." She gave up on the peas and went for her soggy potato instead. I stared at my bean burger in bewilderment. It was generous of the kitchen staff to try and cater for the annoying American vegetarian, but actually as I eyed the rounded brown splodge, part of me wished they hadn't bothered. I'd grabbed a glass of room temperature milk at the serving hatch, so I made do with sipping that down. "Tonight, we are having your welcome party."

I choked on the milk. "A... sorry what did you say?"

"A party? You have those in New York, right?" Phil chuckled to herself. I almost corrected her to Queens again but there wasn't much point.

"Yes, parties are sometimes had in New York." I couldn't help but smile at her. This place was weird, and the people were weirder, but I got her. Something about the crazy Brit spoke to me.

"So, you'll come?"

"The party is for me, right? It would be rude not to."

My eyes swept along the vaulted ceiling. The draft in the hall was penetrable. I didn't think I'd ever been anywhere so dismal and depressing in my life. "I don't blame you for needing a party every so often."

"See, you get it already. It's more a social gathering than a party, but whatever. It keeps us sane." My eyebrows raised into my hairline. I wasn't sure sanity was a viable mental state at Fire Stone, but I bit my tongue.

Phil glanced at my plate. "Aren't you going to eat that?"

"I'm not looking forward to it." The veggie burger was an unappealing, dried-up mess.

"The cooks feelings will be hurt," she slid a hand into the pocket of her blazer. "Here hide it in my hanky."

I watched as she wrapped the burger in a square of cotton and popped it back into her pocket "Buster will want it anyway."

I didn't know what question to ask first. One exploded. "Why on earth do you have a hanky?"

Phil shrugged, "Guess I learnt it from my dad. He always has one shoved in his pocket." She pushed back from her chair and motioned for me to follow, strolling for the exit and back to the sleeping quarters. The day was done—well, apart from the party.

"Who's Buster?" I scrambled to keep up with her determined pace.

"You'll see."

In my room, and alone for the first time all day, I flopped on my bed. Rain was still pelting the window. What a day. The girls seemed nice. Those who recognised me from the cabbage fuelled lunch yesterday had waved and spoken when they'd been able. Everyone was friendly.

There was one glaring omission to this statement.

I closed my eyes, remembering what he'd looked like standing at the door to English; the way his eyes had smouldered like burning coals as they fell on me.

I didn't like him.

I hadn't spoken one word to him. But I didn't like him, and it was nothing to do with the fact my blood boiled, and I wanted to physically hurt him every time he was in sight.

His arrogance rolled off him in waves. I'd seen boys like that before: the jocks on the teams back home, their confidence something innate and inbuilt. They'd popped out of the womb with a smirk on their faces.

Tristan Prince was one of those boys.

With my eyes still closed, I folded my arms resolutely over my chest.

A party? I wasn't sure.

I didn't even know if I wanted to know these people more, seeing I was only going to leave them. I'd learned a long time ago not to grow attached because I never knew where I was going to be next, or how long I had in one place.

This, my trip to Scotland, was supposed to be different. But it wasn't. It was another endless cycle in the life I knew.

Exhaustion tugged on my eyelids and I tried to fight it off. I didn't want to sleep; it was only about five o'clock. I blinked and stretched. I wished I had my phone, so I could do something that didn't involve staring at ancient brick walls. Of course, there were books I'd picked up through my lessons. A history book on Celts sat on the top of the pile. I sat and crossed my legs. Better to read a history book than to fall asleep again at five. I'd never make it to the *social gathering*.

I flicked the pages waiting for something to jump out and grab my attention. It all looked pretty wild and savage. An echo from the horn blown in my morning dream seeped back into my memory and I glanced at the window sure I'd been called. What the hell? There was someone out there? A girl. Was she crazy? With my mouth open, I clambered onto my knees and walked towards it. The handle was stiff again, and I yanked hard, pushing as it squeaked. "Hey," I called when the window was open. Rain splattered on my face. Almost horizontal sheets, the rain was unlike anything I'd seen. "You're going to catch your death out there." I squinted through the mist. The girl stood off in the distance, her white dress catching in the wild wind. Red strands of hair streaming behind her.

"Bloody hell." I turned and looked back into my room. Should I go out there and check she was okay? Could I even make my way outside without getting miserably lost down dark hallways? I turned again to check how far away she was. Maybe I could shout louder?

There was no one there.

"Strange," I muttered, pulling on the window and wiping the rain droplets away with my palm. I could have sworn there was someone standing out there in the torrential downpour.

Now I was wet. And cold. And miserable. I fell onto my back, pushing the Celtic book onto the floor. I thought of going to find Phil, see if she wanted to hang out for a while. But I was cold and cross, so I rolled myself in the blanket and shut my eyes. Maybe sleep would help my mood. Maybe I was still jet lagged? Or maybe it was Fire Stone and the fact I wasn't supposed to be here...?

5

Caledonia

I knelt on the floor crushing herbs. They seeped and stewed, filling the air with hints of sweetness which mingled with the earthy tones, and unfortunate stench of stomach bile.

The festival had been a success. Casting my eyes around the settlement I allowed myself a small grin. The festival had been too much of a success for some.

"Deacon, you suffer?" My voice was far louder than necessary, and I chuckled as he clutched his head, falling onto a wooden stool by my side.

"Priestess, you tease." He winced instead of smiling and pushed his greasy blonde hair back from his eyes.

"Father's mead is potent, I don't know when you will all realise." I nudged my knuckles against his knee, bashing him gently with humour.

"Next time I'll realise, it's a promise." He stopped talking and spent a couple of moments groaning, with his skin tingeing green. "Help me please, Mae, I've got to rethatch two hut roofs today. I don't want to be climbing feeling as sickly as I am."

I smiled and stirred the herbs in the pot as I simmered them over a low flame. "Here, lean over the steam and breathe it in."

Deacon's sleep smudged face crumpled, and he rubbed at his brow. "Inhale the steam? Are you sure?"

"Yes, try it. I promise it will help."

He shook his head and then cringed when he realised it hurt far more than keeping still. "What will you folk think of next?"

I stifled another light laugh and pulled him forward so that his face drifted in the light steam curling the air. "We shall think of lots of things to make you feel better when you've overindulged."

I watched closely, waiting to see if my concoction worked the way I expected it to. Herb lore was the only part of my training I enjoyed—if I could get it right, it would make it much more worthwhile. As if by magic, the spearmint and camomile worked, clearing his head with clarifying mint and soothing yellow flowers. Eventually, his colour returned to almost normal. His body relaxed, the creases on his youthful forehead smoothing as his headache lessened.

"I haven't seen Tristram this break of fast." I kept my voice light and nonchalant. It didn't stop him cracking open an eye and smirking.

"Do you intend to ease his headache too?"

I narrowed my eyes. "No, I believe he can suffer."

Deacon chortled to himself, no longer clutching his head with the movement. "You care for him really."

"That giant oaf? Sadly, it's my job to care, but I shan't ease his suffering if he allows himself to get into such a state as last night."

Tristram had celebrated the capture of the deer and the feast we were able to provide a little too well. I eyed his father's large round house. There had been no movement. Either he was truly feeling dire or...

I straightened and smoothed my skirts leaving Deacon to benefit from my herbal concoction. Taking a roundabout way along the outer edge of the settlement, I attempted to glance in to Glynis' small hut. It was just her and Tristram who hadn't risen to face the new day. Even the smell of the remains of the deer cooking to make a stock hadn't made him rise, and I knew nothing moved him faster than the call of his stomach rumbling.

Glynis had made her availability all too obvious to Tristram. While I'd had to sit there watching, glaring, burning with annoyance.

I tutted and scowled in the direction of his hut. I'd spent too long allowing my mind to wander in Tristram's direction. I should have been focusing on my studies; not the broad sweep of his golden-skinned shoulders. I kicked at the dirt with the heel of my sandal.

As was the right in most of our neighbouring tribes, a woman of age could choose any man she desired. Glynis had made her choice very clear, and full of mead and that awful brew his elder brother had concocted, Tristram had been glowing under her advances.

"Gah." I hated him. Sometimes. No, most of the time.

"Looking for someone?" Heather tapped my elbow and peered up at me. Short and stocky, she had that natural build woman of her profession required. Thick strong forearms were all the better to pull a new bairn out of a woman's centre. I cringed. The blood and mess of yesterday was still uncomfortably raw.

"No." I frowned again at Tristram's closed door. If

Glynis was in there with him, wrapped in those golden brawny arms of his, I would never talk to him again—not in this life or the next. Well apart from when I had to as his Priestess—but that was it.

"May I have a word with you, My Baduri?"

"Of course. Is everything okay with the bairn?"

Heather guided me away from the settlement, weaving towards the tilled ground waiting for life to grow. I frowned at the soil. It seemed stark and unforgiving. I made a mental note to speak to Father about the lack of crops and new growth and turned my attention to the rough-skinned woman at my side. Her quick bright gaze was focused on my face and I shifted uncomfortably under her frank appraisal. Her greying hair was braided, and decorated with blue gems, and at her throat a dark-blue crystal the size of an eyeball settled in a copper disk. I had no idea how old she was, she was just Heather.

"Heather, is everything okay?" I thought of that little scrap of crying flesh we'd coaxed from Agnese's womb. It would be a tragedy if some misfortune had fallen on him during the night; there would also be a lot of unnecessary sore heads this morning too.

Guiding me to a log, out of view from the rest of the villagers, she sat on the rough bark and patted the space next to her. "You did well yesterday, Mae."

I offered her a tight smile. "I only did what little I could, as I have no skill in such matters." I shifted uncomfortably, not ready to discuss the golden flow which seemed to spread through my veins, running in my blood as quick as water. "She was fortunate to have you there." I placed my hand over the top of Heather's, her weathered skin was smooth and dry under my touch. "We are always lucky to have you assist us."

Heather gave me a small smile. "I feel like I may not be around to help for much longer."

I swept an alarmed glance over her. She seemed to be fighting fit to me. "Don't talk nonsense, Heather, you can't scare me like that."

She turned her face towards the trees of the forest. The trees were drooping, their leaves turning with the chilled autumnal weather. "You will be eighteen soon. Time to choose yourself a man and embrace your position within our hierarchy."

I contemplated Tristram's closed door and pressed my lips into a tight line.

"I've got a lot of studying to do, many years ahead of me before I can consider things like that. I want to do the best by my people."

"Little Priestess, I believe you've more coming to you than you expect." When she turned to me, her eyes shifted with power, like ice floating over one of our ancient sacred lakes.

"I'm not that little." I smiled. I couldn't help but wonder what she wanted to talk to me about. We seemed to be skirting around an unspoken conversation. Recalling the golden flow of energy, I wasn't sure it was a conversation I wanted to have.

"Here, take this." She thrust something into my hand, curling my fingers over a hard object.

"What is it? Why are you being so mysterious?" A nervous laugh bubbled in my throat.

"It will help... with the connection."

"Connection? You mean training?" I opened my fingers and gazed at a purple rock screwed onto a metal hook. It hung from a fine chain.

She shrugged. "Who knows what I mean? I'm an old

lady given to fancies, but I do believe you are very special."
She clasped her hands in her lap and gazed up at the sky. I
followed her line of sight. Swift clouds moved with the
autumnal breeze across a horizon of the brightest blue. "I'll
be glad to soar high again; this mortal plane has become
wearing," she said.

I smiled. "You will soon come back when your time in
this life is over. Your skills are much needed; your soul will
live again." A sudden urge moved my hand to squeeze hers.

She shrugged, her shoulder nudging mine. "Maybe, but
then maybe I've fulfilled my role now." Her quick gaze
settled on my face for a brief moment before lifting again to
the sky and the gods above.

"Maybe, but I think not." A rolling churn squeezed my
stomach. The thought of change, even the passing of the
Kneel Woman, caused my throat to tighten.

Her next question caught me unawares. "Who will your
soul search for in the next life, Mae?"

My thoughts instantly ran to Tristram, swept on a wave
of golden energy. As angry as I was about the previous
evening, my mind instantly delved to where I held him in my
heart.

If I shut my eyes, I could see him. Sometimes he was all
I could see and dream about. But around the constant he
provided, as annoying and childish as he could be, there
was a dim dark cloud. I couldn't believe I could ever
choose him as mine. There was no explanation why; I just
sensed it. If I probed into my future, there was nothing
other than a dark abyss of nothing. Never more had I
wanted my training to be over, so I could control the sight
like my father did. Then I'd know. Then I'd know what my
destiny held for me.

"Thanks for the stone," I turned to Heather, starting with

surprise when her space was filled with fresh air and the Knee Woman was nowhere in sight.

I turned the purple gem in my hand. It wasn't one I recognised—yet another example of how far in my lore training I still had to travel. I sighed. The Kneel Woman was known for her cryptic ramblings, but we all smiled and let her get on with it, after all she was the one who guided most new life into the settlement with little tragedy. But a jewel? With a shrug, I popped the chain over my head. If it helped with my studies, I wasn't going to dismiss it. In fact I'd never take the thing off—I needed all the help I could get. The earth gave us many tools, and stones and crystals were essential for multiple tasks. Maybe this was the crystal of remembrance, in which case I needed it more than any other.

I sighed and sat for a moment. It was quiet, calm out there at the furthest edge of the settlement. Behind me the forest stood and waited. Would it provide more food today? Turning on the log I searched into the trees. Withering beech trees shook their golden leaves at me and I smiled at their pretty dance. Behind them a solid oak, the tree of our people, loomed large and strong. Like the tree, so tall and proud, our people would never fall—I'd make sure of it, even if took me countless years to learn how to help them.

I closed my eyes, relaxing with every breath. To wander in one's own mind was a great achievement. There was a place you could find where you could just be, the future stretching before you, the past settled, drifting with the sands of time—unchangeable and complete.

Meditation was a challenge. My brain didn't want to settle, my thoughts never wanted to still. Every time I cleared my mind, another thought would jump in. How was I supposed to expand my foresight, if I could find it, due to the endless chatter my own mind created? I was doomed.

Ignoring my nagging self-doubts, I cleared my mind. Then I cleared it again. I focused on the log underneath my dress, refusing to let my brain think of anything other than the old tree and the way its rough surface was scored and lined with age.

The gentle hum of rain falling through leaves caused me to lift my face, expecting to find damp droplets falling. I opened my eyes when no rain fell on my skin. Closing my eyes, I heard it again.

Most strange.

I was happy sitting in the quiet, playing with the sound of rain, when the shout of my name rose loudly from the depths of the village. My stomach dipped when I recognised the voice hollering.

What was I going to do if he was glowing from his time laying with Glynis?

Swallowing a hard lump in my throat, I steeled myself. I would act as any baduri, any priestess, would. I'd treat him, help him, and then I'd shut myself in my hut and curse the day I'd ever laid eyes on him.

I stomped to the central hearth, the scene of the festival last night. The common ground, its fire pit and free space was for the use of everyone. Our settlement was circular, dotted round houses all faced in towards the hearth. Surrounding us, a low brick wall formed an encasement which prevented children wandering, and wild animals venturing in. Behind the wall was the forest and wilds of our land.

Tristram was laid on a plank of wood, clutching his head —still in the same clothes he'd worn the night before. I contemplated the wilds of the forest. I would rather be there than glaring at the man before me.

"My Mae," he clutched at my hand, pulling it tight to his chest, "Why do you allow me to suffer?"

I yanked my hand away and surveyed his face. Golden thick hair covered his jaw, the skin under his eye shadowed. "You did this to yourself," I replied, my voice sharp.

Unable to help myself, I glanced at Glynis' door which was still shut. I relaxed a little but not entirely.

"Come help me, Mae. Deacon said you cured his ails." His eyes were screwed closed, his long fingers working the bridge of his straight nose.

"Maybe Deacon didn't suffer as bad as you because he didn't partake in all the many things you did."

With his fingers still squeezing the skin between his fair brows, one eye popped open, and he levered onto an elbow, wincing as he moved. "And what exactly do you think I partook in?" His skin turned to an ashen hue and he fell back. "This is your father's fault, that honey wine is unnecessarily strong."

I smirked. "I think the man who overindulges is the one to blame, not the man who made it."

Tristram groaned and mumbled something about magic which I dutifully ignored.

Sighing and muttering under my breath, I went to the fire and scooped up a bowl of bubbling water. Clear and scorching, the liquid slopped in the earthenware vessel as I reached into the leather belt around my waist. A gift from my father, the belt contained a pocket in which I could keep my sacred herbs. Herb Lore was by far my most enjoyable study.

I added the spearmint and camomile, the same as Deacon's ague lifting stew. I turned back for Tristram, finding him now dozing, a gentle snore emitting from him. With deft fingers, I dove back into my pocket and grabbed a bunch of tied herbs, dropping it in the water. Casting a swift glance over my shoulder, I ensured Father wasn't close at hand. He'd smell the unique notes of the herbs I was using. Powerful and potent, Foxglove was rarely used unless by a skilled hand. I'd seen father use it once on a wandering member of a neighbouring tribe; the man had been near senseless as he'd admitted he hadn't been lost at all, but instead spying. I kicked at the remnants of the fire from the previous evening and snatched a clump of charcoal into my hand, dropping it into the water.

As I walked back to Tristram with my potion carefully balanced in my hands, I broke every Druid Lore code, but with a narrow stare at Tristram's face, relaxed in the repose of sleep, I steeled myself for breaking the law.

I wanted to know the truth. If he'd given into Glynis' considerable charms, then it would change everything. I placed the bowl seeping the truth-expanding Foxglove and Charcoal under his head and sat on my haunches waiting for him to come around once again. Settling back on my heels I watched and waited. It only took a few minutes for the tight rivet of pain settled between Tristram's eyebrows to smooth away. In many ways, it was a shame; he should have suffered longer. I shook my head at my own spiteful thoughts and I waited.

He cranked an eyelid, the dark shimmer of his onyx pupils settling on where I sat. "Don't sit there looking all virtuous, Mae," he grumbled. "Gloating doesn't suit you."

I narrowed my eyes, making the corners of his lips hitch upwards before he closed his eyes again with a deep sigh. "Some of us have to be virtuous and abstain from the downfall of men, especially if they are to nurse the suffering the following day."

He pulled a face which if my stomach hadn't been

twisted into knots of apprehension would have been on the border of adorable.

"Tell me." He didn't bother to open his eyes to converse with me. It was better that way, at least his soul appraising dark eyes couldn't spear my heart from their brutal depths. "Don't you just want to have fun once in a while? You've the rest of your life to be the bard, teacher, and healer you are destined to be."

I swallowed hard. His words pinched at my chest, labouring my breath. Turning his head, he slowly blinked his eyes open and stared at me. Around us, the settlement evaporated into a fine mist. I breathed slowly, watching as his chest rose and fell in time with mine.

"Have I stumped you into silence, Mae?" He grinned and the magic around us broke into fractured pieces.

"Do you ever plan to be anything other than an aimless second son, with nothing more to do than be the life of the party?" I snapped, sending the hardest glare I could summon in his direction.

The smile on his face evaporated. "If that's my destiny, then so be it." His face shut off from mine and he turned away, his expression hardening.

I knelt forward, coming close to his side. Prone on his back, with his face to the sky, and his eyes shut, I was able to sweep my keen gaze along his features. The boy I'd grown up with had developed into a fine young man. At twenty, his still youthful body contained power and grace. He'd been blessed by the gods at birth. I studied the sweep of his golden eyebrows, the regal slope of his nose, and the wide plump lips I hoped hadn't kissed Glynis. "Don't you want to be more, something undeniable by anyone else, to be your own destiny?" I whispered, unsure if he was asleep again. His eyes met mine.

"Always." His words were a low murmur.

"Then you will be the man I think you can be."

"And you?" he asked, "don't you want to be more than a bard? More than the path your father is encouraging you along?" He shifted onto his side, lying close to where I sat cross-legged. Again, that magical spell pulled away reality, absorbing the past and future until only the present remained.

"Always," I whispered back.

His hand reached for mine, his fingers tangling loosely, and my heart pounded against the bones in my ribs. "My head feels much better, thank you, Mae."

I offered him a wan smile. "I'm here to heal."

In a surprising flash, he pushed my hand to his chest. My palm sat above his beating heart, the force of his existence in this life. "You make me live, Mae." He squeezed my fingers and my own heart raced. "I will live every day being more than an aimless second son, if you would allow me. If you would take me for your own."

My mouth dried. I pulled my hand away, shoving it within the folds of my dress. "Who did you sleep with last night?" The question blurted between us with no hope of me holding it back.

Leaning onto his elbows he frowned in consternation. "What do you mean?"

The mist of truth-giving steam swirled around us both. "Did you sleep alone?"

His features hardened into a bitter scowl. "You think so little of me?" He sat up, his muscles flexing as he stood from where he lay. He began to walk away, his head down, before coming to a standstill and casting a hooded gaze back in my direction. "And to think I'd give the world for you."

"Tristram, wait, I didn't—" there was no point calling.

He was gone, storming across the settlement. I shook my head, frowning at the earth. Nothing about this was easy. I wanted his laughter, his affection, his love. So why did it feel like I had a mountain to climb to achieve those things?

I should have chased him. Apologised. Instead, I blinked back stinging tears.

I kicked at the bowl of herbs. Stupid things were supposed to make him talk, not me.

6

A wet smack hit my face, and I waved at it with one hand. "Ugh." Hot air fluttered across my skin, followed by another swipe of warm stickiness.

My head throbbed, the dream... it had... there weren't words to explain it. I opened my eyes, wincing when they stung like I hadn't slept in a week. I glanced at Phil looming over my bed. Next to her, with two giant paws pressed into my chest, winding the air out of my lungs, was a giant dog.

"What is that?" I attempted to shift from under the canine's weight, but it wasn't to be budged. With a groan, I gave up trying and waited to be rescued—hopefully before I stopped breathing. "And why on earth is it in my room?" The remnants of sleep and the intense, absorbing dream were still chasing away, but I could tell by the chill against my skin I was in room thirteen of Fire Stone. For a moment, an ache for the familiarity of Queens surged through me. People would be on the street, sirens would be wailing, it would all be comfortably familiar.

Here, there was silence, rain—and excessively large dogs.

"It's Buster, he says you're missing the party." Phil had no worries about breezing into my room and waking me up. It was as if it were the most natural thing in the world to her, but to me it was alien. Foster homes were neutral spaces, with each care kid carving out their own niche of space which wasn't to be violated.

I stared up into the face of the dog. Even his whiskers were huge and splattered with giant drops of dribble. "Hey, Buster? Any chance you can move?" Breathing was becoming an issue. Not that I was bothered about breathing right now as dog breath fanned over my face with meaty undertones. I tried not to gag.

With a broad sweeping wag of his tail he jumped, spring-boarding off my chest. I cried and struggled to sit up before he could attack me again.

I blinked and struggled to get my bearings. As the chill had assured me, it was room thirteen all right, but the draughty space was hazy with shadows. Was it morning already? No, it couldn't be. I'd only been reading a few moments before.

"What time is it? How can the party still be going on?" I flung my hand out patting for my watch. Not having a cell phone sucked. It was like going back generations by having to do something as banal as checking a watch for the time.

"Seven thirty?" I blinked at the watch again, but the hands didn't change. "I haven't been asleep that long?" Although... that dream, it seemed to go on for days.

Phil nodded, her curls shaking like petals caught in the wind. Moving to the window she pulled at the handle, yanking it back into its frame. "How the hell did you get that open?"

I shrugged and flung my feet over the edge of the bed, although the stone floor was so cold I wished I hadn't bothered pretty damn quick. "I didn't." Buster sat and watched with large expectant eyes. "I don't have any treats," I told him. "They only serve cabbage here."

Phil snorted and turned from the window, reaching down to scratch Buster behind the ear. "He's used to cabbage, he's adapted."

I shook my head and tried to find a low gear I could crank myself awake from. Everything was muddled. That dream, those dark eyes. No amount of head shaking was going to erase them from my memory. Yawning, I stretched high, my body creaking from where I'd slept so soundly, not moving. "It feels like I've been asleep for ages."

"Are you going to keep falling asleep instead of getting ready for our social extravaganzas?" She quirked an eyebrow at my dishevelled appearance. "Look at you!"

I glanced down. My uniform was rumpled and dirty, like I'd been running through trees. "What? How the hell did that happen?"

Phil grinned. "Welcome to Fire Stone. Weird shit always happens here."

My blood chilled. "What do you mean by weird shit?"

Buster licked my hand, and I scratched his glossy black fur. I didn't know what breed he was, but his fur was silky, and he was fricking enormous.

Phil shrugged and perched on the end of my bed, waving her fingers towards the dark wood wardrobe. I shuffled over and pulled out a tank and some skinny jeans. They felt oddly comforting and familiar in my hands after wearing the strange uniform. I shucked out of the skirt and draped it across the back of the wooden chair, unbuttoning the stiff white shirt and flinging it in the corner. "Nice housekeeping, I like your style." Phil nodded at my laundry pile of underwear.

"I try hard." I grinned at her, the sleepy fog easing from my mind. As I blinked, I still caught a hint of those jet edged eyes, as if they were imprinted on the inside of my own eyelids, but the fogginess I'd woken with was lifting. "What happens at these parties?"

"One of the boys has contraband goods." Phil studied her fingers, picking something out from under a nail and flicking it onto my bedroom floor. It was gross on so many levels.

"What sort of contraband?"

She shrugged but I could see an irrepressible smile curving her lips. "Booze, fags, that kind of thing."

I pursed my lips and narrowed my eyes until she giggled. "Booze, and cigarettes."

"Yuck." I'd only got drunk once before, not that I was some well-behaved prissy princess, but alcohol did nasty things to my stomach. It wasn't worth the vomiting.

"I'm joking." She paused before adding, "Well there might be beer."

"I thought the boys and girls were in separate wings?" I pulled at my ponytail, flicking my head upside down and scraping my fingers through the reddish chestnut strands before tying it back up again, this time into a messy bun I secured with pins. The moment it was up, errant red wisps instantly fell down. It wasn't worth the fight to tease them back up again—my hair had its own agenda which I was never a part of.

Patting the bed, she told Buster to jump up.

"Phil, don't do that, he will make it all slobbery and hairy." She pulled a face and glanced at the bedsheets. Under closer investigation I could see he'd already managed to make them hairy and disgusting. I narrowed my eyes at him as he circled four times on the mattress before creasing his giant body into a ball and positioning himself directly on my pillow. "Thanks, Buster."

"He likes you; he doesn't sleep on just anyone's pillow." She snorted and pushed her glasses up her nose.

I appraised the dog who was now licking his ass on my white pillowcase. "Really?"

"Nah, not really." She waved her hand in circles and dramatically groaned a bored yawn. "Come on, we haven't got all night, all the good stuff will be gone."

I checked myself with a sweeping glance in the mirror. My blood froze as I blinked at the reflection staring back at me. What was that?

I chuckled nervously as I glanced down and double checked my dark jeans and white stretch tank.

There was a very good chance I was losing my mind.

"Happy?" Phil asked oblivious to my trembling.

"Sure." I turned my back on the mirror, my heart pounding. My fingers shook as I grabbed my room key and slid it into the pocket of my jeans.

That wasn't what I'd seen when I'd looked in the mirror. I'd seen her. The girl from my dream. Hair all wild tangles, her dress bedraggled, and a red cape's hood covering half her face—my face.

"Where is this party?" I jogged to keep up with Phil's determined step. A gentle bass of music thumped from somewhere on our floor. "It's not here in our dorm is it?"

Phil grinned, her eyes alighting with mischief. "Of course, we are where all the best parties are at."

"As opposed to...?" Her hand reached the door of room two. From under the doorway bright coloured lights pulsed.

"The boy's dorm. We take it in turns."

My stomach twisted with a nasty stab. My hands clenched into tight fists and the thud of my heart in my chest deafened whatever Phil was saying. Her mouth moved, glossy lip balm catching the dim glow of the hallway, but I couldn't hear her above the boom, boom, boom, settled within my rib cage.

"Who brings the contraband goods?" I shouted as if I were at a club and couldn't hear over the music, but I knew who she was going to say, even before her lips formed the first letter. My hands curled ready to throw a first punch.

"Tristan, of course." She pushed on the door and ice filled every cell in my body. Of course, it was him.

His gaze was locked on the door as it opened as if he expected me the way I already knew he was there. His hand, clutching a plastic cup, froze midway to his mouth. The flimsy plastic gave way under his tightened grip, and knots of muscle strained in his neck as his eyes fixed on where I stood on the threshold.

"Come on, Mae, let's get a drink." Phil slinked into the room. From my peripheral vision, I sensed it was packed—bodies moving with the beat of the music. But unable to focus on anyone but him I stayed rooted to the spot. Phil left me at the doorway as she threw herself into the party, calling out her welcome to all the nameless faces watching us arrive. Buster sat at my feet, a deep rumbling growl vibrating through his fur against my leg.

"Phil, I can't," I called, to tell her I couldn't enter, couldn't stay. Couldn't do anything apart from want to fly through the air and rip at Tristan Prince's skin with my fingernails, but his voice cut through the air.

It rang like a clear sharp note. Speaking straight to my pounding heart. "Don't worry. I'm going." My eyesight dimmed with every vowel and consonant he muttered. He wasn't even shouting over the noise of the music—I could just hear him, as clear as if he were stood next to me whispering in my ear.

Ripples of hostility scored the air.

Horrified, I rooted still. The fact I hated him impulsively was one thing. That was my inexplicable issue. The fact he clearly felt the same about me, was something else.

He brushed past my almost frozen form in the doorway, his arm skimming the chilled skin of my arm. Pounds of furious anger mingling with an unknown quality rushed through me at the touch of our skin. It burned, and I jumped out of the way.

We'd never even spoken, yet he was going to walk out again, just like he had in English.

Like shit he was.

I paced after him, surprised at how much floor space he'd cleared in the time I'd been frozen and stuck. "Hey," I shouted, but he didn't slow down. His wide shoulders, and burnished gold hair stormed to the end of the corridor and down a winding staircase. The moment his head dipped from sight, the furious rage within me subsided.

Hesitating, I glanced back at the party where my new friend was probably having a whale of a time, drinking some illicit contraband delight.

Contraband bought by Tristan.

"Damn." I cursed and began to sprint, skidding down the steps. A far-off door slammed and I barrelled towards it.

I pushed through a door finding only another empty corridor on the other side. "Shit."

"Stay away from me."

I jumped at the vicious chilled blast with which the words were spat. Wheeling around I found myself directly in the space of Tristan Prince. His face, so proud and aloof, contorted into a vehement mask.

I opened my mouth to speak but instead, I flew at him. My hands gripped at his arms, fingernails digging into his flesh. "I haven't been anywhere near you." My face folded itself into a painful unfamiliar scowl.

Shock dashed in his eyes before they hardened. Deep, dark, hardened flints... of... of... onyx and jet.

"I hate you." His aggravated statement hammered somewhere in the depths of my stomach.

"Not as much as I hate you."

Still clutching one another with vice-like grips we stared hard. If I could have laser-beamed and melted his brain with my gaze, I would have without a second thought. Deep down I knew this was crazy, but the overwhelming feelings of hatred towards him overrode my common sense.

"You've never met me." His lips curled into a twisting sneer.

"Thank God, you repulse me." I shuddered. The intense sensations made me want to puke.

His hands tightened on my shoulders, my bones aching under his crushing touch. "You need to get away before I hurt you." He leaned closer, and I inhaled the scent of earth and fresh air. My head whirled with nausea. "I will kill you, right now, with no hesitation." His icy statement should have had me running for help, calling the police maybe? I didn't move.

I sneered, curling my top lip like a ferocious lioness. "You hurt me? You'd never be quick enough."

I wanted to stop myself speaking. This wasn't me. I wasn't this person. I'd never so much as trod on a spider. But the boiling rage pushed the words out of my mouth like a molten volcano.

"I will kill you," he repeated. His hands skimmed from my shoulder, along the skin of my neck until his long strong fingers slid effortlessly around my throat. I swallowed, my face heating with lack of oxygen. He *was* going to kill me. I thrashed with my hands, then my feet, kicking and thrusting, trying to make contact, all the while he held me. His dark furious gaze settled on my burning face.

"Tristram." The name came from nowhere. My eyes closing as darkness flickered around the very edges of my being. From the place where they'd been tattooed onto the inside of my eyelids, I sought the dark gaze from my dream. I found them, although they were dotted with stars, the lack of oxygen making blood vessels burst. As unconsciousness pulled me along a teetering edge between here and the expanse of space before life ends, I searched for that dream. For the hand clutching my hand to a firm chest, the air rushing and rising, pulling two bodies towards one another.

We were stood under the trees. Birds chattered and flapped as though they watched us and approved. "I love you, Tristram, you know that." I blinked into midnight eyes. "You'd never hurt me, not even for my blood."

I pressed against his chest with one last feeble effort.

Except it was her hand... not mine.

Not mine.

"Tristram," I gasped. It was the last word I'd ever say. In my heart, it etched a stencilled outline which told me it was my first.

He was gone. His hands leaving my skin. His footsteps echoed like a racing heartbeat down the hallway. I gasped and clutched at my throat, gagging and heaving. Sweat tingled along the back of my neck. Falling to the floor, I placed my hands and knees on the hard flagstones, breathing hoarsely. He was going to kill me. But I knew I would have done the same if I'd been bigger and stronger.

What the hell was going on?

Crawling, I made my way to the doorway at the end of the corridor. A green sign pointed a white printed 'Fire Exit' at me. Still on my knees, I pushed at the door, willing it to open. But I wasn't strong enough, I wasn't strong enough for anything. I slumped against it as I allowed darkness to take me.

I'd go anywhere to be away from him.

I remembered the jet eyes as I slid under. Wouldn't I go anywhere to see them?

Another wet slobbering lick bought me too and I sunk my fingers into the deep fur along Buster's back. "Are you on a rescue mission?" I whispered to the dog. Opening my eyes, I blinked into woodland. A wet nose nudged my hand, pushing me to get up.

How did I get outside?

I smoothed Buster's fur. "Let me rest a few minutes. I'll be fine I promise."

With my eyes shut, I listened to the rustle of leaves on the trees; crisp and dry they were preparing to fall. I loved this time of the year, the golden hue of the glowing trees always reminded me of his hair. He'd come back, he always came back when he was sent on errands, although he'd never left after we'd spoken cross words before. I patted his dog and nestled further to the ground. Just a little sleep, no one would mind.

"Mae!" The call stopped me from slipping into the deep sleep I craved.

"Coming, Father." With an internal sigh which made

my stomach dip I forced my eyes open. Instead of trees I found only a shadowy ceiling.

"Mae, what the hell happened to you?" It was Phil who stepped up close, her face creased and pale.

"Nothing, I got lost." I staggered from the floor. My whole body ached as if I'd been hit by a truck.

Her fingers gingerly touched the skin of my neck and I winced as she prodded the bruised inflamed flesh. "You got lost? Mae, it's midnight, you've been gone for ages."

Her words didn't make any sense, but I clutched onto her arm. "Help me get back, I need to sleep. I can't find my way along these ridiculous hallways."

Phil nibbled on her bottom lip, her eyebrows knitted together. "I think we should go and find Mrs Cox. She's a cow, but she'll help. You've been attacked or something. Don't you remember?"

I shook my head—although it was a lie. The jet and onyx eyes, hardened with hatred, teased me from behind my lashes. "No, I've just got lost and fallen, let's get back." I tried to smile at her in the dim light but couldn't quite rally the sentiment to work its way to my lips. "Come on, Phil, you know me well enough to know I need to sleep."

Still unsure she glanced about. "Okay, but tomorrow you promise to tell me what happened?"

"Sure?" I lied smoothly.

I wouldn't be able to tell her anything. I didn't under-stand what was happening. My dreams and reality seemed to be merging into one confusing mirage of the improbable.

I followed her, leaning my weight just slightly on her arm.

I wanted to know where he was.

After everything I still wanted to find out where Tristan Prince was.

Seared in my mind was the image of the man from my dreams. They were two of the same; there was no denying the startling similarity. The same, except one was full of love and mischief, and the other filled with hate and violence.

I sunk into my bedsheets after Phil had navigated me back. I'd run a long way after him, into a part of the house I hadn't ventured before. The party was over, all the lights dim.

Please don't let me dream. I almost wept with my prayer.

Please don't let me see him again. It would hurt all the more seeing the finer, gentler version, when I'd wake knowing the hateful dark imitation would still be under the same roof.

7

Caledonia

I searched for Father in the mist. The new day had risen: fresh and damp. Tendrils of swirling smoke mingled with the foggy gloom, dragging the sky down upon our heads. The chilled fingers of winter crept with stealth towards the golden hue of autumn, stealing its glory for another year. Breathing in deeply, I watched the settlement. Women warmed water in pots over the fire as children pulled on their linen dresses, needy and loud. The rich smell of bread weaved through the air. Baking day was my favourite. Men scattered along the circular edge, busy with their jobs. One was whittling wood into sharpened edges. Turning my head, I caught sight of the smithy and his son bent over smelting metal as they bashed with solid tools. The men completed their work around the edges of the large settlement, not through accident, but out of design. This was a time of uneasy peace, the agreement with Druia of the nearest clan made our homes a little safer. But no agreement was stood to last. Change was afoot, even the smallest child could sense it, without the skill of sight my father controlled. We were hungry, food was scarce, our supplies low. A sharpened edge chiselled the features of every member of our tribe. Gods, how I hated these times. Within my heart a burning need to do something to help flourished into a fire of flames.

These times... closing my eyes, my fingers wandered to the purple gem resting against my skin. A deep sense of unsettling unease spread from my chest to my stomach, balling itself into a hot knot of unrest. I attempted to clear my head to try to see an image of what faced us, but only blankness and the call of the cries around me met my efforts. With a sigh, I gave up—which described most of my training to date.

"Mae, are you ill?"

I fluttered my eyes open and found the pale worried gaze of Alana quizzing me. She stepped closer and ran a motherly touch along my forehead. I clutched her hand and squeezed it tight. Our roles seemed to have reversed. I was the elder, yet she was the one with the parental instincts I didn't possess. Although I was only days from being eighteen, the prospect of having a child of my own seemed as unfamiliar as the foreign language of the travellers who sometimes passed through to trade with Alen.

"I'm fine, Sister, just a little tired," I said, offering her a weary smile. A cloak of exhaustion and apathy seemed to be settled on my shoulders. I couldn't shake it off or discover its source. Yet in a way, I felt as though I was stretched too far, like the dough the baker women were kneading by the hearth. "Maybe I'm trying too hard with my meditation. Trying to be quiet isn't a skill I possess."

She frowned, the sharp line dipping between her eyebrows temporarily corrupting her regal air. "You and *father* are both distracted and tired. I don't know what you hope to achieve with no sleep."

"Sleep?" I darted a quizzical glance in her direction. "I'm sleeping like a log—in fact when I'm sleeping is the only time my mind is empty." I grinned and punched her lightly on the arm, but it didn't lift her mood.

"You've been talking in your sleep for days, tossing and turning." The blue of her gaze lightened. "It's a wonder anyone in the settlement is getting sleep between you and Agnese's new bairn." She sighed and turned for the hut and I followed her back inside. Hit by the musty taint to the air after the freshness of outside, I stalked for the window, and opened the shutters wide, allowing light to stream in. All the huts within the settlement were similar, round and basic, but ours was a fraction grander than the others, with two bedrooms and storage space for our cooking chattels. It was home, but if you looked too closely you'd see the touches missing which our mother's skill and instinct would have made complete. As always when I thought of mother, my chest caved a little with the weight of knowing she was gone from this life. Lore and teachings told us we'd see her again, but I didn't know who I was looking for—her face was shadowed by forgetfulness, an image evaporating with time. The familiar panic that I wouldn't see her again settled around my chest. "I miss her too." Alana interrupted my thoughts.

"Mother? You can't remember her, surely? Even my own recollections are hazy."

"I can feel where she would be." Alana's touchingly simple statement made my eyes prickle.

Smiling, I poured a cup of water for Alana and passed it towards her. "Me too. I wonder if Father would have been different if she were here?"

Alana sipped her drink with a delicacy I didn't

possess. I glugged mine, much like the men of the village had glugged father's honey wine the other evening. "He seems so distracted. I remember as a child," I went to interrupt her to remind her she was still a child, but the dreaminess which stole over her expression stopped me, and I listened intently. "I always thought he was the greatest warrior, watching him walk with his staff and sword, commanding the village." A troubled cloud passed across her pale face. "Now he mutters and frets, constantly distracted. Worried more with words than the actions of protecting us."

"Alen and his sons protect us too." My mouth dried a little at the thought of Tristram and his elder brother. Two men, both very, very different. I knew where my preference laid, even if he was as annoying as a yapping puppy.

Alana's pale gaze met mine and she worried her bottom lip between her teeth. "It's not the same, Mae, and you know it. The bard should lead, guide us with skill and wisdom. Lead us fearlessly into the unknown future." She hesitated. "I know I may not understand it, probably never will, but Father doesn't seem to be connected to us the way he once was."

I mulled over her words. Could I even remember the last time I'd seen him? Spoken to him for any length of time? He left me to the training of Amargen and Elion, two skilled bards who knew their lore and practice, but who had never harnessed the power my father controlled—or had controlled, if my sister's perceptions were to be believed. "He seems to be amongst the oak trees a lot. Maybe he's calling for help? Who knows what he can see; his power is his own." I wasn't really trying to soothe her worry. I knew Father's mind could wander. We would never understand what he saw or strived to attain for us.

"I worry." She twisted her dress between her fingers and gently I eased it from her grasp.

"I think you are the one with the skills of the bard, not me."

Her wildflower eyes settled on my face. "It's you, Mae, it's always been you. Father has never had any doubt that the skill of our people would run in your veins."

I stared at my hands turning them over. I could sense no skill, no power. Nothing other than confusion and frustration that I couldn't remember a single thing of my training. Throwing off the depressing thoughts, I clutched the gem under the neckline of my dress.

"Come, cheer yourself," I said, offering a wide smile. "I'll go find Father and see what I can find."

She laughed. "He won't tell you anything. He's as wily as a quarry in front of the hunt."

At the mention of the hunt, my stomach rumbled. "We could do with more good fortune like the deer the other day. I hate for Alen to order a hunt, but we can't carry on with these levels of supplies."

Alana cocked an eyebrow and her lips curved. "I'm sure if there is a hunt, there you will be, two steps dutifully behind Tristram, watching his back for wild boar or stray arrows."

"As is my duty as baduri."

A snort lifted from her wrinkled-up nose. "Of course, Sister."

She smiled, her pale lips curving and transforming her face from pretty to beautiful. "Maybe Father is praying to the gods, so you don't have to go hunting with Tristram again."

Grinning, I turned her to the door. "Maybe. He'd be much happier if I dedicated the time to my studies."

I waved her off, and she went to go gather the children ready to give them their lessons, setting them on the damp earth in a circle so she could tell them stories of old magic and the gods. I watched for a while, frowning at the scrawny appearance of the children. Bread wasn't enough to feed these little mites. Not the loaves we had the ingredients to bake. They needed meat, and more than one doe could provide. Alen would again send a hunting party out, this time maybe for days. I'd joked with Alana, but there was no way Father would allow me to go with them to help.

I shook my head. Tristram had avoided me the last few days since our words over the potent steam, but the thought of him wrestling a wild boar turned my stomach.

A shouted giggle from one of Alana's little charges spurred me forward, and I went in search of Father, turning my mind off from wasteful thoughts of Tristram.

"Father?" I'd walked the woods under the safety of the oak trees. Still within the borders of our lands I kept my eyes peeled for any unusual activity. Other clans sometimes wandered our way. Sometimes traders. Sometimes people with immoral intentions. We hadn't been raided since I was a child, although what had happened that night no one spoke of.

A sigh of relief escaped my lips when I caught sight of Father. Standing on a dais of vibrant green weeds, under a crowning oak tree, he looked magnificent, and I paused to enjoy the sight of him. What it would be like to have his knowledge? To have his skills? I didn't even know how far his true skills went and I was his eldest daughter training to follow him. The life of a bard, of the high priest, was one of mystery and speculation. Some bard's in history, so Elion had told me, could read the minds of others. I didn't know if Father could. I'd never been brave enough to ask.

I startled when another man walked from the trees.

Impulsively, I dropped to my knees so I remained out of sight. Alen walked up to Father. Too far away, their conversation was muted, but father waved his hand around at the majestic oaks, pointing to numerous trees. Alen followed his indicating gestures, concentrating deep in thought, his face stony and hard.

Disharmony ran between the two clan leaders—I didn't need to be a fully trained baduri to read that much.

Crawling forward, and straining to hear, I slunk through the tall weeds and grass. "It's the perfect position. I've watched the stars for many nights, the alignment is strongest here."

Alen shook his head. "But these trees, they've kept our ancestors' safe, they've provided a home for our settlement—"

"And now I shall provide something stronger. Something that will stand still even when we are nothing but dust blowing in the wind, and the stars are still above the ground on which our footsteps have long been unable to walk."

Father turned, and I dropped lower, holding in a gasp with the palm of my hand. His face was taut and haggard, his deep eyes set within hollowed prominent bones. He hadn't looked like that a couple of days ago? Had he?

They discussed a delivery, expected within a few days, and then Alen walked off, back towards the settlement, his back ramrod straight.

I paused a moment, unwilling for Father to know I'd been eavesdropping, but before I could straighten and feign a natural arrival, he spoke. "Mae, I know you're there."

Struggling from the ground but dropping my eyes, I walked towards him, picking a path over the knotted weeds and uneven earth. "Father, I didn't mean to eavesdrop. I was coming to find you."

I met his gaze, scared to face the haggard man I'd seen talking to Alen. Frowning, I saw only the face I'd always known. A little aged in places, hair white and flowing. The ghostly glimmer I'd caught from my spot in the weeds was gone. "Father, your face. You looked so ill when I caught a vision of you a moment ago."

Father settled deep-blue eyes on my own. "Just a shadow, Mae. You shouldn't look for things that aren't there."

"Alana is worried you're overtired. You aren't sleeping or eating."

"You girls, you need to stop harassing me." His words were light, but a fast and testy undercurrent flowed through them. "I'm fine, it's a worrying time. Things are changing, can you sense it, Mae?" He cast his astute gaze back onto my face. "Some new enemy approaches, Alen's scouts have heard of devastation in the south of the isle." His fingers drifted to his beard as they always did. I didn't have a beard to stroke, thank the Gods, but I did have my pendant and with his words it began to hum against my chest. Fathers quick gaze flitted over me. Strangely, I was glad the pendant was hidden beneath my cotton dress, out of the way of his sharp assessment. "This army that approaches, it leaves devastation in its wake and ensnares the peoples of the south as slaves."

I shuddered and again the pendant vibrated against my skin. "They won't get here though. The clans will unite and rebel."

Father stared at the sky as if he could still see the stars. "Maybe." When he turned to me his face was etched with hardness. "Or maybe each clan will clamour over each other as they try to be the ones who survive."

I swallowed hard. Would our people end at the hands of an invading army? My feet shifted in the earth and I had to restrain myself from running back and raising the warning.

If we packed up now, we could leave, make into the wilds of the hills and the forests. We would be hidden there, unnoticeable. There was nothing at the settlement we couldn't leave behind—apart from one another.

I lowered my head and breathed. It wasn't my place to act without the say of my liege or my priest.

"What were you talking to Alen about, Father?" I changed the subject in the hope of averting Father's disapproving and thoughtful gaze from my face. "You know you can trust me." There was a weighted pause, and I bristled like a scolded child. "You can. I know you have your council and I know there is a hierarchy, but I am your daughter and one day I will be trained. One day it could be me who stands alongside our leader and makes the decision." I had to stop myself from adding another maybe onto the end of my statement. I knew the day was far off, if not never arriving. But I had to brazen it out. Had to make it seem like I knew more than I did—that my training and hours spent with my tutors wasn't for nothing.

Father stared long and hard at me, reading my eyes. I fought a nervous twitch and stood still and proud. "One day, Mae, you will surpass us all."

"I don't know about that," I stuttered. Was he mad? Maybe his foresight was waning if he thought I was the one who would truly be gifted with our lore. I almost cracked a smile, ready to goad him into admitting he was joking. His face was stern and sombre, and I paused, a tremble aching in my tummy.

"If you focused and stopped worrying about what that oafish infantile second son is doing."

I nearly snorted but kept it in check; instead I flushed a deep burning red. "We've been friends since before we could walk. Of course I worry about Tristram. What sort of baduri would I be if I didn't?" Father would see through my flimsy excuse, but I chanced it anyway. His face flushed a florid red and his hand tightened on his staff. I watched the battle waging inside him to tether his emotions down. No one disobeyed my father. I would for Tristram though—it was instinctive and written in my heart.

He shook his head. "You waste your time."

I straightened up, pushing my shoulders back. "Maybe. But then who knows?" I squinted my eyes and tried to read him the way he could so easily see me. I failed. "Anything could happen, and I will always protect all of our settlement, whether that's the smallest child, or the oafish second son of our leader." My cheeks stung pink and I pushed a hand at my hair which seemed to cling to my face.

Father paused. Silent. It frustrated me no end how he would drive an argument, dropping it at his will, regardless if I had finished my say or not.

"Alen is going to send him to assess the threat."

The ground tilted beneath my feet and I flung a hand out to the side grasping nothing, to steady myself.

"No! He can't. It's too dangerous." I shouldn't have spoken. Father's face closed and folded. "There are others surely?" I stepped up, reaching for him.

He held up his hand, and I muted my torrent of reasons why anyone other than Tristram should be sent on the journey South.

We stood separated by a silent wall of disagreement.

"What of the trees, Father? What were you saying to Alen?" If I were given to fancy, I could imagine the trees leaning overhead, listening, as though they also wanted to hear his answer.

"We are going to chop them down. I'm building a new

temple to the gods. We need all the help we can get in these dark times."

I stared up at the trees, so tall and stately. Sentinels keeping watch. "The trees? But they are essential, they are part of us." I shook my head fast. This must be a joke?

His steely gaze laded on my face. No softening was to be found in his features. There was no humour to be found. "Now we need something else."

"There is nothing else," I said. "The trees give us life, protection. The old ways are tied deep within their roots."

We were disturbed by the crash of approaching footsteps. Two men stepped forward, their faces fearful as they carefully held their axes close to their bodies. "Ah," my father greeted. "And here come the woodsmen," he turned to me. "It's time for change, Mae. Be ready for it."

Turning on my heel, my feet flew through the grass and weeds. I wanted no part of the beautiful life-giving trees being murdered. I wanted no part of any of my father's plans.

I ran until I could no longer breathe.

The glistening waters of the lake winked with familiarity. Shadowed by brooding mountains the crystal mirror reflected the sky and clouds above. The mist had lifted to a clear, crisp day, but over my heart a fog heavier than any swirling tendrils bringing morning dew hung heavy. I'd ventured too far from the settlement, but the thought of seeing my father, the tree killer, made my pulse thud. I didn't want to return there to see that. And more so I didn't want the people of the settlement to look at me with expectation in their faces that I could explain what he was doing.

What was he doing?

What temple? We'd never had a temple before. All our ceremonies and celebrations were held under the green canopy nature provided. Anything more than that seemed unnecessary.

Settling on the bank of the lake, I unstrapped my sandals and edged my toes into the water. It was gasp-inducing cold, and my murmured exclamation set birds chattering in the nearby forest. Relaxing, I closed my eyes, trying to ignore the plight of the trees weighing heavy on my heart. What was father thinking? Trees were sacred, they fed us knowledge and power. I wasn't alone in knowing this. What must my tutors be saying? But like me, they knew not to argue with the chief bard. His law was the law of the land. Chief's came and went, but the bards would always stay. Our power came from the earth, from nature itself; some even whispered the Gods. My power had not arrived yet. I was a long way off from unlocking the knowledge within me, if ever. My journey to enlightenment was only just commencing, but I knew what could come. No one knew how their knowledge would manifest—it just would—with enough study and training we might wield great power.

Old stories spoke of bards who lived countless generations, their longevity a gift given from the ground in reward for dedication and skill. Those days had passed. Blood and power had mixed with untrained men and women, spreading the skills of the Druid law, but diluting the strength of those who wielded it. My father's skills and powers were exceptional. I could only hope to reach a level like that.

Tristram's words circled back into my mind. With my eyes closed I meditated on them. Was I happy with my Druid training, or did I want something more? Could I be the best Druid I could be, and serve the people with all of myself, if my heart belonged to him?

I snapped my eyes open.

My hand clasped the pendant and my toes stretched out into the cool water. For a long while I sat, happy to be, content to listen to the lap of the water.

Tight fingers held my throat, squeezing the life out of my lungs. I struggled, grappling against the grasp. Searching the face burning at mine with hatred, I reeled when I found black jet eyes glittering with malevolence. "Tristram," I gasped his name, clawing for breath. My feet and hands lashed with no impact.

"Tristram."

The blast of a horn shook me awake, and I blinked into the darkening sky. With a shiver, I sat up. My feet were frozen in the frigid water. Searching blindly, I sought out Tristram. Angry as he was after our row the other morning he wouldn't hurt me. I was sure of it.

Tell that to my racing heart. My legs wobbled as I stood. The horn blasted again, and I turned for the settlement. Hitching my dress, I ran, my hair catching on trees and tangling into knots. I told myself I left the nightmarish dream behind on the shores of the sacred lake, but I hadn't. Its ghost followed me into the village and smack into the chest of my childhood friend. "Mae?" His gruff greeting zapped shivers along my spine and I trembled, holding in a scream, fearful of what man I'd find in front of me. The Tristram of my childhood or the apparition who'd hurt me, wanted to kill me, in my dream?

"You're scared? What's happened?" He softened his stance, shifting closer. The silence he'd been treating me with evaporated into the deep honey warmth of his voice which melted my bones. His chin lifted as he glanced over my shoulder, his hands protectively sliding along my shoulders. I quivered beneath his touch.

"Just a dream." My words shook like one of the leaves of the forest about to fall for winter.

"A dream?" His wide lips quirked into a smile. "Don't let dreams chase you, Mae." His whispered breath fluttered over my skin and the depths of my tummy began to heat. An inexplicable burning ran through my stomach down to my toes.

"It was you. You were hurting me." I trembled.

Deft fingers swept along my brow, tucking a tangled curl behind my ear. "I'd never hurt you."

Our gazes locked, and my breath stole through my mouth on ragged gasps.

"Mae, what's wrong? You look like you've seen a ghost." Alana called out and picking up her skirts of her dress she ran towards us. The whole settlement milled around. Amargen frowned when he saw me. I dropped my gaze. I'd missed yet another day of training. At this rate it would take me fifty years to train instead of the standard twenty. I'd be dead before I became a Druid.

I shivered, remembering the hands around my neck.

Tristram made room for Alana but he didn't relinquish his occupancy of the space nearest me. "I'm fine, Alana. It was silly, I went to the lake and fell asleep."

Tristram hissed, his dark eyes burning. "You fell asleep by the lake? Mae," he admonished. "Anything could have happened to you."

I shrugged and laughed, although it sounded laboured and unnatural. "It's the lake. I go there all the time."

Tristram's stance was stiff, his hands balled into fists, the muscles of his arms bulging. "Well, Baduri, now you won't." His face closed off and I reeled at his use of my official title.

He'd never called me anything other than Mae, even when it became clear I'd follow in my father's footsteps.

"What's going on?" Tristram marched away, kicking dirt in his wake, so I focused my question on Alana. Her face was pale, her lips bruised where she'd been practising her bad habit of chewing them. "Alana?"

"There's an army marching north." She clutched my hand.

"How do we know?" Silently, I sought out Tristram's broad shoulders. He was still here, but according to my father's news he was the scout being sent to seek out news.

"Because refugees from the borderlands have come." Her voice wobbled. "You should see them, Mae. Children. Just children." She broke off, biting on her lip with such ferocity a bead of blood gathered next to her tooth.

Letting go of her fingers, I marched towards Tristram who stood with Deacon, Alen, and my father. "What's going on?" I demanded.

Father's eyes met mine. "Our end." He didn't flinch with his words and I could only focus on one thing, Tristram's dark tortured gaze meeting mine.

8

My throat ached as I swallowed the weak coffee. Running a finger along the edge of the collar on my cotton shirt, I kept my wincing to an absolute minimum. Phil was already watching me with hawk eyes, although she'd insisted she wouldn't tell anyone else. I'd only been here a couple of days, I didn't need to be the focal point of gossip for the rich kids abandoned to this hellish place.

I couldn't stop thinking about Tristan Prince. It was obsessive. I'd woken from my dark dreams thinking of him. He'd tried to kill me, but I still wanted to see him. I should be talking to the school or the police. Why wasn't I? It was messed up on so many levels. Wasn't that a thing? Stockholm syndrome or something? Maybe I'd call it Fire Stone syndrome.

His eyes and their furious black gaze were haunting me through every moment.

I glanced at Phil. "Can I ask a question?" The silence between us was unsettling and I couldn't bear it another moment.

Phil raised her eyes from her porridge and gave an encouraging nod.

"Are your dreams weird here?" I studied my coffee to hide the blush tingling along my cheeks.

She chewed thoughtfully, although what she was chewing on considering the porridge resembled wallpaper paste, I didn't know. "What do you mean?" She slopped another spoonful towards her mouth and I swallowed. The last thing I wanted was food. I could have done with the coffee being ten times stronger.

"I don't know. Since I've got here, my sleep seems all messed up, my dreams are exhausting. In them I'm always outside, always in the forest. It's like I'm being battered by nature. I always dream of the same people..." I stopped myself from saying *man*. My face flushed brighter and I returned my stare to the table. "Forget it, I'm just tired."

Phil kicked me under the table and I glanced up. She was pulling a silly face and googly eyes. I chuckled despite the hideous embarrassment. Her face dropped, and she lowered her voice. "Well, my parents brought me here originally when they were working. I told you that, right?"

"Yeah?" I nodded and sat up, offering her a small, grateful smile. I'd never met anyone like her. I couldn't help but wonder what my childhood would have been like with her by my side as my wing woman, instead of always being the weird foster kid.

She carried on. "They were searching the grounds and forest for an ancient settlement that's rumoured to be here."

"And?" Philomena was drawing this out, I hoped it would end somewhere exciting and informative.

"Well, nothing was found. But the records hint that something was here. So, the conclusion all those boring-as-hell experts decided on was that the castle itself is on top of where the settlement must have been."

I frowned and mulled over this. "That can't be right, there would be other clues: scattered pottery, stray animal bones."

Phil raised an eyebrow and then pretended to yawn. "You should meet my parents, you'd get on like a storm."

"Maybe I will." I gave her another smile. "When are they coming back?"

She shrugged, and I took a sip of my coffee, shifting my gaze as she frowned, lips downturned at her breakfast. "Anyway." She shook out her curls. "So, from what I unfortunately was forced to overhear as I died a slow and painful demise due to extreme boredom, was that no one can understand what's happened. You," she wagged her finger at me, "are right. It's like magic. The castle has absorbed everything, or everything else has disappeared."

"Magic?" A creeping tingle crawled along my spine. I ignored it. Magic was stupid made-up shit little girls believed in.

She shrugged again as she shoved a spoonful of runny, lump-filled liquid into her mouth.

"Doesn't explain my dreams though." I was too scared to close my eyes in case I saw the same people again. The girl and... *him.*

"Maybe it's ghosts?"

The crawling shiver from my spine spread over my skin. I couldn't allow myself to think of the similarities between Tristan 'I'm such a Psychopath' Prince, and the man from my dreams.

"What is it?" Phil peered closer.

"Nothing." I wanted to tell her, but I held back. It was too crazy.

The only rational explanation I had was that it must be the dislike Tristan Prince and I mutually held for one another causing my dreams. That was logical. Ordered. I could categorize it and file it somewhere in my 'Don't Open' box.

Logical... I think I abandoned that when I stepped out of the limo on my first day here.

Maybe I could speak to Tristan, try to sort out this irrational hatred we seemed to have developed without even communicating with one another. My throat ached where his hands had squeezed the air out of me. Then there was that incessant tug to go find him. Would we talk if I were to track him down? Would we fly at one another, hurt one another, kill one another... or would we kiss?

This was the moment my stability teetered over the edge.

I couldn't stay here like this. I was exhausted, unrested, and I'd been attacked. If that could happen in the first three days, what hope was there for the following weeks? "I'm going to go and speak to Mrs Cox." Impulsively, I pushed from my chair.

"What about?" Phil went to stand after me, but I held out my hand to stop her and she hovered an inch out of her plastic seat.

"How long I have to stay in this place before I'm allowed to leave." I turned on my heel telling myself her crestfallen face didn't hurt the way it really did.

My rap on Mrs Cox's door was met with a cheery, "Come in." I straightened myself up and tried to look like I meant business as I pushed my way through.

Her office still smelled of toast, which was more than the students in the great hall were getting.

I was determined that if I ever got out of here and into the town Phil had mentioned we could go to, I'd use what little money I had to buy a cheap toaster and some sliced bread. Before I starved to death.

She was sitting behind her desk, but she stood when I entered. My eyes automatically flickered to the tapestry of the stones and then back to her.

"Ah, Mae, and to what do I owe the pleasure of this morning call?" Although her skirt was immaculate, she smoothed at the material with her hands. Next to her I looked ungainly and like I'd just dived straight out of a dumpster. "I assume everything is okay? Mrs Barlow says you have a passionate view on Shakespeare."

I flushed, the wind taken out of my sails. "I don't think that's true," I stuttered. Next to her gentle Scottish burr, I sounded brash and sharp. It hurt my own ears to even hear my voice.

"Oh, Mrs Barlow is an excellent judge of character." She peered over the rim of her glasses, her quick gaze searching my appearance. "Are you okay, Mae? You know in the absence of your aunt you can speak to me about anything." She slipped back into a giant leather chair behind her desk, almost disappearing into it. Coughing, I perched on the visitor chair where I'd sat and eaten my toast only a couple of days before. Time was odd here. It seemed I'd been here forever. I hadn't. I'd only really made one friend, with no more time to meet other people and talk to them—my welcome party had been an epic fail.

But then wasn't it the dreams at night making my days here seem longer than they were?

"Actually, that's what I was coming to ask you." I gasped in a quick breath for luck. "See, I was wondering when my aunt would come back. I just, I just don't know if this is the place for me. I'm not sleeping well, I'm tired, and it seems insane to just thrust myself into a school when I don't even need to be here." My words ran on with no pause. With a calming deep breath, I slowed my pulse and tried to speak evenly. "I was happy to come and visit, but I had no idea I was coming here, to a school. And everyone is lovely, but..." All I could see was Tristan. That unfounded need to find him burned and sizzled in my veins. I ran out of words. What more could I say without sending up a red flag and alerting the teachers to the fact I might need psychiatric help?

Mrs Cox was out of her chair and patting a comforting hand on my arm in record time. "It's just jet lag, Mae. You must hang in there; this is where you are supposed to be." She perched on the arm of the visitor chair and gave me a squeeze. I'd never had a teacher hug me—not ever. Was that even allowed?

"Says who? My aunt? I haven't even met her yet. Why are you so keen for me to stay?" The question, once I'd formed it, made sense. Since I'd arrived, Mrs Cox had been sure that I was supposed to be here. But why? So Tristan 'I'm Such an Ass' Prince could kill me down a dark hallway? Or so I could starve on porridge, and lose my mind to repetitive, almost on the point of real, dreams?

To my horror my eyes stung. I blinked them away. I didn't cry. I gave up crying a long time ago.

"Listen, Mae, your aunt is a very busy woman, but she will be here soon. How about I try to get in contact with her and see if you can speak? I'm sure everything will be clearer once you've talked to her."

When I'd opened the letter from my long-lost aunt, I

hadn't known what to think. If I was being honest, I'd been hoping for someone cool and caring, like Peter Parker's aunt, someone like that.

Not a blank space.

Not a faceless signature on a letter.

I stood, my legs oddly reluctant. "I'll give it a week, then I'm out of here."

"We will sort it." She stood and reached a hand for my arm giving me a hearty squeeze. "I promise. I know you've been lost, Mae, but this is your home. It's where you belong."

I walked for the door, my heart down by my shoes. I turned and found her watching my departure, a thoughtful expression on her face. "I've never belonged anywhere. This is just another place to add to the list."

The thought of going to class filled me with dread. My feet scuffed over the stone floor. I stared about me, an absorbing wave of apprehension pulling me down. I didn't want to be in this dark godforsaken building. Its damp chill was oppressive and stealing the air from my lungs. What I wanted was to feel the sun on my face; the air: breezy and warm. What I wanted to be was home—but I didn't have one of those. I didn't even have a way to contact the people I'd left behind. I should have asked Mrs Cox for access to my cell, maybe she would have relented if I'd told her how desperate I was for normality.

The kids here, they seemed to think this was all normal. That schools were dull and drab, the lighting dim. That dreams were chased with dark tormentors, maybe even ghosts.

Phil was something else. The friendship she'd extended

to me filled me with some comfort but even she seemed happy shovelling porridge in her mouth and going along with the eccentricities of the place.

I mean, we weren't even allowed outside.

A rebellious urge began to grow. With my head down and my feet speeding to a moderate jog, I dashed for the arched doorway I'd been guided through by Mrs Cox. Fresh air tantalised my skin, droplets of fine rain splashing along my hair. It was heaven.

Ducking around the side of the building, I followed the gravel path, stepping in shallow puddles and splashing my bare legs. Now I knew why Phil asked if I needed to borrow gum boots. I didn't care. The water sloshed in my shoes and I squelched away quite happy. Outside it was just as I'd imagined. Fresh, green... alive. At the edge of the manicured grass, the forest waited.

Greedily, I sucked at the damp air. My skin glistened with the light misty rain, and as I walked, I lifted my face to the sky, closing my eyes and allowing nature to heal the disappointment darkening my soul.

My aunt didn't want me.

It was the same story I'd always known. "Be a good girl, Mae, and behave." Or, "Do as you're told."

A frustrated ball of annoyance settled itself under my ribcage. I'd been stupid, hasty. I should have found out more before I got on the plane. If I'd known the full truth of where I was coming, I would have used the airplane ticket and then dodged Jeffries in his chauffeur cap, at the airport. I could have been anywhere by now, be anyone. Instead, here I was in a navy uniform with bruises around my neck.

This was me though: impulsive and hasty. I wouldn't be me if I hadn't accepted the plane ticket and dove headfirst into what was offered.

"Mae!" I recognised Phil's voice, but I didn't want to stop and chat. If I didn't stay out of that building and find out what was on the outside, I was going to suffocate. With my head down, I marched down the pathway.

There weren't any further gardens apart from the short stretch of grass around the stone walls, not that I could see through the grey mist and hazy rain droplets. The paths gave way to wild forest. The house was surrounded around the back, the trees encroaching on the space of the building. Peering into the trees, I sought out a path ahead. The closer I got to the dark trunks and vibrant greens, the lighter I felt. This was freedom. Grinning, I lurched forward into the deep foliage. Wet ferns slapped at my legs and my feet squelched in mud and soft earth. With every step my breath became lighter, my heart thrumming, free from the cage of anxiety restricting my rib cage.

Peering up, I sought the top of the trees. Spiralling high until they touched the sky, they provided a sturdy canopy from the light rain and I managed to pass under the leaves relatively unscathed from the wet elements; apart from when a large droplet would gather and roll off a leaf, splatting onto the top of my head.

I didn't care.

The trees pulled me deeper. Further. Until I rounded into a clearing and found him.

He didn't see me. I stopped, teetering on the spot. An instant rush of bile hurled up my throat.

Why was he here? I wanted to be the only one out here in the freedom providing woods. His broad shoulders were turned to me, his golden hair glinting in the leaf diffused clearing. Bent over a sketch pad, Tristan Prince's attention, thankfully, was focused on his piece of paper. I froze, unable to move, a deer trapped between the headlights of a murderous, careening truck.

Turn away, my survival instinct screamed as my throat pulsed, the bruises from our meeting only hours before, still stiffening my flesh.

But, I couldn't. I wasn't given to homicidal tendencies, but I stepped closer, and then closer again. That same intense desire I'd felt even as he stalked away from me the night before took over. That pull I'd had in Mrs Cox's office to go in search of him—it was there, inside of me. Deep within the centre of my body, the need to search for him abated.

I still wanted to stab him with a pole and parade him at the entrance to the nearest bridge. The two opposing forces warred within me.

Although I was silent in my approach, his shoulders stiffened. "Don't come any closer." With his quiet words, my legs trembled and wobbled.

My chest tightened until every breath stung. Yet still I stood there. The trees waved and watched as awkward silence spun around us. I scanned the page his hand rested on. Sensitive pencil strokes had drawn the leaves hanging overhead. How could the fingers that had nearly squeezed the life from me have produced such a sensitive and light touch? I gasped. Under the leaves was me, outlined in slate grey. Same eyes, same nose and lips. Only my dress was different. In the place of the trainers and skinny jeans I'd worn the night before was a simple cotton dress which hung to the floor, hinting at the curves I kept safely hidden beneath layers of baggy outerwear.

The forest began to darken, stealing shadows creeping into the edges of my vision.

I took an instinctive step towards him. The pulsing

repulsion which made me want to hurl sharp objects at him, jarred against the need to know what it was about this place, about those repetitive dreams.

"Don't come closer," he repeated, and my stomach flipped and dived like on the rollercoaster at Coney Island. I clutched my tummy.

"Why are you drawing me?" I edged an inch forward as he snapped the cover over his drawing.

"I said stay away. Have you got a death wish?"

"Have you?" I sneered a little, the anger and hatred taking over from my curiosity. "You tried to kill me last night. Who says I would have shown the restraint to walk away?"

He had walked away the night before. Now I was seeing him here, the night before focused into a clearer picture. Somehow, he'd managed to walk away before he'd actually killed me. That thought lit a spark of realization. What was I supposed to feel? Gratitude? What was that turning my stomach, at war with the hatred?

The tendons in his neck knotted, a dark flush burning under his tanned skin.

"We can't be near one another, Mae." The way he said my name made my mouth go dry.

"Why?" Another step.

His eyes flickered in my direction and the pain in my tummy intensified until it felt like I was being stabbed with a kitchen knife. I glanced down to check I wasn't bleeding out.

He was almost shaking, his skin white, his hands clenched so tight the pencil in his grasp snapped. With the rise and fall of his shoulders, any hope I might have irrationally held that he would answer me was dashed. "Because I want to kill you." He turned then, and the mask on his face was a split between furious repulsion and anguish.

"Why?" My fingers shook. My feet were telling me to run.

"I don't know." I wished I couldn't see his face with its desolate confusion.

"Do you hate all Americans you meet?" His smouldering dark gaze ate away at my insides.

"Just you." He turned, breaking off our conversation. Using all my efforts, I managed to move my feet away from his spot in the wooded grove, the whole time mumbling about his dickwad behaviour. A few paces away, I hesitated as he swung back around. "You'll thank me for not killing you."

I pulled a face: infantile and ridiculous. Honest, if I had to live in this place much longer I might take him up on his offer.

Mae. I chided myself. I'd lived through the accident which had killed my family. Life shouldn't be joked about. Especially not when you'd nearly been strangled to death the night before.

I turned and found him staring at my retreating form. We watched one another for a long moment until my heart ached as though it were bruised. Then I ran.

I ran so hard, blindly flying through the trees. Droplets of rain mixed with my tears against my cheeks. I hated this place. I wasn't meant to be here. It was hell. I'd rather be back in Queens with a fake family and boyfriend, than here with the dreams, and him, and...

I fell to my knees, a twisted root of a tree pulling me down onto the soft mushy earth. "Shit." I rubbed at the nasty gash scored across my kneecap. This was why stupid school uniform skirts shouldn't be worn.

I kicked at the tree root with my foot. "Thanks." I grimaced and winced trying to roll my weight onto my uninjured leg. Glancing around me, I looked for any markers of where I was. What I was expecting I didn't know. A goddamn sign post—*way back to hell here?* There weren't any signposts. There wasn't anything apart from trees, clouds, and damp shit everywhere. My dramatic sigh made my shoulders shake, and I collapsed sideways into the dirt, holding my knee up to investigate. Me and blood weren't the best of friends, so after a bit of deep breathing and general head wooziness I figured it was best to cover it back up again and just let the germs and dirt do their thing.

Like an upturned beetle, I rolled onto my back, allowing my head to rest on leaves, twigs, and unlimited piles of worm shit. The thought of porridge in the great hall was incredibly appealing, not helped by the fact my stomach was growling from missing breakfast.

My hand touched the root of the tree. Thick and sinewy ropes spread out like clutching fingers. Travelling my gaze from the roots I sought out the tree which had tripped me up. It was hard to tell, they were all so close together, tightly clustered as if they were hiding something.

I screamed when a prod moved my leg. Scrambling back, I glanced, searching out some rabid wildlife, lurking, ready to eat me alive. But it was just me and the trees.

"Crap," I grumbled under my breath. *I need to get out of here.* The only other person I knew in these woods was someone who wanted to kill me.

Cursing and muttering, I rolled over onto my knees, expecting the deep cut to sting like a bitch. I was glancing down to find out why it hadn't hurt when I was thrust forward head first into the gathering of tight trees by a sharp push from behind.

With a screech, I toppled forward, landing in ivy and small, white wild roses. Scrambling, my hands scraping on sharp thorns, I staggered to stand. Winded and with my pulse thumping in my veins, I turned to find who'd attacked me. I thought it would be Prince. Unable to resist, who'd come to finish what he'd failed to do the night before.

It was the trees.

Crazy. But the only things around, despite me straining to see anything else which would make logical sense, were trees. They were closer, tighter, suffocating. A soft tap nudged my foot and I glanced down, a scream ripping from my lungs.

A long bone lay across my foot. Shrieking, I turned, trying to run away, but the trees were too tight, blocking any available path. My hands flung to the side as I tried to keep my balance, my fingers landing on a smooth hard surface beneath the ivy. "What the hell?" My exclamation was strangled and muted by the wall of green trapping me in. Ignoring the bone as best I could, which was near on impossible, I brushed at the ivy, peeling it away in grasping fists. The stone was smooth and grey, ancient and worn, its surface dimpled and scored.

With my heart racing, I cleared the clinging weeds and flowers until the long rectangle of solid rock was free from its covering. Scrambling, I pulled at some more as sweat dripped down my face and I dashed at it with my arm. The trees watched on as I cleared the stones. Five of them; they were like the stones I'd seen once on the History Channel. Similar to the tapestry hanging on Mrs Cox's office wall. Instead of standing proud in a circle, they were tumbled down as if they'd been knocked over by a passing giant. It wasn't the ad hoc positioning that drew my eye. It was the bones. Two human skeletons lay wrapped together tight.

Mae.

I whirled. Who called my name?

With shaking legs and trembling fingers, I crept closer. I should have been screaming and running back for the school, yet the trees seemed to be circling me, supporting me during my gruesome discovery.

Were these what Phil's parents were searching for? Yet I'd found it with no skill. In fact, I'd fallen over them.

Dropping to my knees, I placed my hand on one of the stones. Deep within its surface a deep rumble met my touch.

"Who are you?" I stared at the bones, my hands itching to reach forward and touch them. "Why are you here?"

A faint glimmer from within the tumble of legs and arms shone in a shaft of light, filtering through the green canopied roof.

Mae.

Leaning forward, I held my breath, my entire being suspended as I reached within the depths of the huddled skeletons.

My palm warmed as I gently eased the gem from the depths of its macabre safe. If breathing wasn't automatic, surely I would have forgotten.

It was the necklace from the girl in my dreams. The purple, the violet glimmer, was the exact same shade, undisturbed by time. The chain was darkened but still complete. Like it had happened to myself, I could remember the grey-haired Heather giving it to her. I tried to recall the words the woman had spoken, but they were hazy, muddled, as if I were hearing them from under water.

It was impossible. I'd watched enough archaeological

programmes on the television to know things didn't survive like this. Not buried only under plants.

I dropped it around my neck. The most natural action in the world. The most natural thing I'd ever done.

It hung there, glimmering against my white shirt. Above my head the trees shook their leaves.

Impulsively, I covered the stones and the tragic remains that they contained. I wanted to know who they were. I knew the remains were of the girl I dreamed of, and the boy so similar to Tristan Prince. With a heavy heart, I suspected they hadn't had a happy ending. But how, or why? And why above everything else, was I dreaming about them?

Slow tears dripped down my cheeks as I covered them back up. "I'm sorry." My words seemed to move within more space and when I looked back up, the trees had cleared; the school was in view off into the distance. I patted the stone nearest to me ensuring it was covered. Beneath me a booming powerful rumble met my touch. It called to me.

"I'll be back," I whispered.

Lit with a newfound purpose, I straightened and turned towards the school. I knew I'd find this place again; not that I'd be able to explain it. With a determined step, the first I'd had in a while, I marched for the castle. I was going to find out what happened here. And more than that I was going to find out why I was the one this was happening to.

9

Caledonia

"Mae?" *A low whisper pulled me from my twisted dreams. The violet gem around my neck pulsed gently against my skin, although it's soothing presence didn't stop me from springing upright and preparing to howl a scream. Strong fingers fell across my mouth and trapped my cry.*

"It's me, open your eyes and look."

It was dark, the faintest sliver of dawn light peeking through the edges of the shutters. The tall and broad shape of Tristram moved in the darkness as he sat on the edge of my rushed mattress. I gasped at his proximity, breathless.

"Tristram, you shouldn't be in here." I pulled at the simple shift across my shoulders, gathering it into a bunch around my neck. Beneath the cotton, the skin along my chest flushed at his closeness. "This isn't appropriate." I glanced at the still slumbering form of Alana.

I could sense his cheeky leer in the dark even though I

couldn't see it. "I've seen you wear less." The smile hidden in the shadows teased.

A stern frown creased my brow and I pulled myself together, tugging at the deer hide which had slipped off in the night, placing it back over my legs as extra coverage. "When we were children, yes." With a deep sigh, I rubbed at my eyes. "What are you doing here anyway? I haven't slept a wink."

His fingers groped for mine and squeezed them tight. "Could you not sleep because you were excited for your birthday?"

He was sitting so close, the warm scent of his herb-washed skin and the evocative perfume of fresh air and forest filled my nostrils until I could have drowned in the heavenly smell. "Tristram, you know we can't celebrate our birthdays. These are dangerous times. You are needed here in the camp and should not be being distracted by such frivolous things as how old we are."

A strong silence met my reproof.

"I can be acting chief after I've celebrated with you, Mae," his tone dipped and with it my stomach twisted and turned. The low burn I'd been experiencing lately flared in the pit of my tummy. "Just give me this, and then after that I will be the man everyone needs me to be."

I hesitated for a short moment. "What do you want to do to celebrate?" Why were my veins rushing with heated blood like that? What did I want him to say? My mouth dried with anticipation.

It would have been easy to lean across and kiss him. But I didn't.

"Just an hour, you and me, just like it used to be." He tugged at my hand, pulling me out from under my coverings. Unable to resist and desperate to feel a lightness in my heart which had long since vanished, I slipped out into the chilled air, shivering a little.

"Can you leave, so I can get dressed?" I tried to make my tone tart, but it trembled and his dark eyes swept over my cotton shift.

"Yes, My Baduri." I bristled at his formal title for my role, but his lips quirked into a smile outlined in the dawning day and I relaxed. "Come, Mae, we don't have long." He stole through the door on silent feet.

With the soft closure of the hut's door, I slipped out of my shift, pulling on my undergarments before swiftly tugging my pale grey linen dress over my head, and tying a leather belt low on my hips. My better dress, I knew it highlighted the speckled dashes of colour in my eyes. My hair, I allowed to fall free and wild over my shoulders. I didn't have time to brush a bone comb through it now. It took hours at the best of times, and I preferred the wild natural look to the infinite pain and boredom of the daily brushing.

With a cast away glance at Alana, who even managed to look beautiful in sleep, I stole after Tristram into the silver dawn.

He was standing in the shadows, his attention focused on some distant thoughts. His face chiselled into a serious expression. An expression I'd come to know well over the last couple of weeks.

"Greetings." I smoothed at my hair as I reached him. His eyes floated over my appearance, a ghosting smile lifting his sombre mood. "Again."

"Greetings."

"Where are we going?" The most beautiful silence hung over the settlement. Even the chickens and what few animals we had were still slumbering. The dawn held a deep chill and I shivered.

"Here?" He stooped to the floor, where he had a basket laden with items obscured under a thick woollen blanket. With sure movements, he picked up the blanket and tossed it around my shoulders. Tugging the edges tight together his face watched mine and we stared at one another for so long my tongue began to tingle with dryness. I coughed, breaking the moment.

"What's in the basket?"

He was quiet. Maybe the tranquil dawn had stolen his boisterous mirth, or maybe it was a culmination of the last couple of weeks taking its toll. Either way his watchful silence made me fidget and pull at loose strands of wool in the blanket.

"Breakfast. Come, Mae, let's share a birthday breakfast before our days give way to the celebration of the people."

I frowned and clucked my dry tongue against the roof of my mouth. "I told you I didn't want to celebrate today; it's not right with the threat we are under."

He leant closer and that wonderful earthy, herb-filled scent washed over me. "What's not right is you not enjoying your day. Come. This is a festival of celebration and I won't hear anything else about it."

"My father would argue."

He chuckled and plucked at my hand, linking his fingers easily within mine like he always had since early childhood. Alen had on numerous occasions in the past taken great mirth in retelling stories of our childhood infatuation with one another and how we used to run about the place with our hands tightly clasped. Those days seemed but a distant memory. A fond memory, but distant nonetheless. "Your father would argue about most things."

Narrowing my eyes, I tugged his arm until he'd look at me. He was picking a path towards the forest, his feet sure and firm on the wet ground. "What have you been asking my father?"

It could have been the sun edging over the horizon, but a pale-pink hint of colour spread across his cheeks.

"Just normal chief and priest discussions."

"Tristram? What aren't you telling me?" That unsettled feeling I seemed to be living with of late squeezed my chest.

His dark gaze swept in my direction and my stomach tightened a little. "Has he not spoken to you?"

I sighed, and we walked in silence for a while. "I've hardly seen him. He seems more distracted than ever. I keep trying to find him to tell him of my studies but he's never where he ought to be." I trailed off, my mind wandering as I replayed the last few days in my head. "He's obsessed with the delivery of stones." I turned towards Tristram. "I don't think it's healthy. Those trees, they hold so much power, he shouldn't have cut them down like that."

Tristram pulled me closer. "Shh, Mae, you mustn't speak like that."

I laughed but his darted glare cut the mirth short on my lips. "Everyone's asleep, Tris." I glanced around at the silent settlement and giggled, but it faltered on my lips when I took in the serious expression Tristram wore. "No one is going to hear."

His lips set into a grim line, the full wide mouth always so quick to smile and tease turned down at the edges. "There is always someone listening."

"What's happening, Tristram? You can trust me with everything, you know that." Why did I seem to be in the dark? Tristram and I, even when he annoyed the life out of me, always shared everything. Why did I now feel that was no longer the case?

The dark onyx of his gaze lifted with a spark of light and

he nodded, pulling on my hand and tucking me closer to his side. My breath caught a little as our hips brushed. "I know I can, but come, this is just us, let's not ruin it with dour talk and worries."

I smiled, but I didn't feel it in my heart. Worry spread a dark cloud over my eighteenth birthday.

"The river?" I looked around in amazement. It had been a while since I'd had the time to come to this favourite place and the dark weight on my heart lifted and soared. Autumn winds and high tides made the river run and churl with muddied swollen water. I didn't care, I knew the water wasn't dirty. This river was the flow from which my people lived. Skipping forward, my heart light and carefree, I slipped out of my sandals and placed my big toe in the water. "She's cold today."

Tristram laughed, the worry I'd watched him carry on his shoulders during the walk here lifting. The dawn was rising bright. Pale golden streaks of sunlight landed on his skin, painting it with a deep glow, making his hair catch a light with pale flames. "Always a she with you."

"I told you," I giggled a little, a careless sound in the morning quiet. "She told me who she was."

Shaking his head, he stepped closer. I held my breath for his touch, but it didn't come. "And I keep telling you, this river must be male, look at how masculine and virile it is."

I chuckled harder. "Virile?" I prodded him with my middle finger smack in the middle of his stomach. It met with firm resistance. "Virile? You sound like Deacon now. Isn't that what he's always telling the eligible ladies?"

Tristram snorted, his arm resting casually over my shoulders. "It's what he tells himself most of the time." A flicker darkened his gaze. "Yet he wonders why he can't get Arethia with child."

Deacon's wife was young, only my age, and they'd been married a good few months. "It will happen when the gods will it."

With heavy lids, he gazed upon my face, "It seems we are waiting for the gods to answer a lot at the moment."

Automatically, and unwittingly, I brushed my fingers through the strands of his golden hair, tucking it behind his ear. "What troubles you, Tristram? Lighten your heart to me, we are old friends."

I hesitated. So much of me wanted us to be more. The violet gem at my throat heated and thrummed. My fingers dropped from Tristram's hair and clutched the pendant. It was silly, but I was sure it was trying to tell me something.

Tristram's attention dropped to the necklace. "Who gave you that?" His tone was guarded, and I prickled.

"Heather. She said it would help guide me on my studies."

Using two fingers he stroked the pendant with a delicate touch. The gem thrummed with energy. "That witch? Who knows what she intends."

"Heather isn't a witch; she's highly skilled, and essential for our people. We'd be lost without her and be a few bairns the less without her guidance and wisdom." I glared at him brazenly, my cheeks heating.

His hand caught mine, turning it palm up, his finger tracing a pattern across my skin. My breath caught in my chest. "I heard you were the one who saved Aggy's baby."

"No." I shook my head firmly. "I was just there."

He continued to trace the tantalising pattern across my skin and my head whirled a little. "What was it like?"

"What?"

"Watching a child come into this life."

I paused. My eyes met his. "Wonderful."

"You know..." His words rumbled with gravel and I held my breath. "I've realised I've taken so much for granted in my life."

I nodded for him to continue. All my words were trapped in my throat.

"With my father and Eernid always being around." He shook his head. "I don't know why they left me in charge. I should have gone to gauge the threat; they should have stayed here with the people who need them."

"And what of the people who need you?"

He snorted, a bitter and soul crushing sound. "I don't think many people need me, Mae."

Placing my hands on his chest I searched his face. "I do."

I wanted to say so much more. Wanted to tell him every dream from within me. To tell him he was the only one I thought of, even when my thoughts should have been focused on other things.

Clasping my hands, he lifted them to his lips. "I'm scared of the man I need to grow to be."

"Then we grow together. You know." I smiled shyly. "I always thought the stars must have aligned for us both to be born and survive on the same night but years apart." I smiled at a fleeting fond memory of the seven-year-old Tristram taunting the five-year-old me that he'd always be older and wiser. Wiser? I wasn't so sure about that.

"The stars?"

The tone of my voice was low and deep, unlike I'd ever heard it before. "They lead us: their power, their direction. It's the basis for all knowledge." I turned for the river. "They even bring in the ebb and flow of our river. The trees we worship and value reach for them."

He nodded and then lifted his shoulders, thrusting off his melancholy. "Come, Mae, what sort of celebration is this?" Reaching for the blanket on my shoulder he tugged it free. "Are you warm enough without?"

I nodded, once again lost for words. Dumbly, I watched as he spread the blanket on the riverbank. Kneeling, he pulled at the contents of his basket, placing fresh baked rolls and berries onto wooden plates. When he'd finished, he stood, his smile on the border of shy. "It's not much, but it's a celebration at the least. Will you break your fast with me, Mae?"

I nodded and sat alongside him. We ate comfortably, the rush and gurgle of the river removing any silence. The bread baked by the village woman was fragrant with ground herbs. Heavy and dense, we wouldn't be going hungry. "Where did you get the berries?" I asked, rolling a red sphere between my fingers.

"I went foraging." He popped one into his own mouth and I longingly watched his lips as he chewed and swallowed.

"Are you going to poison us with wild fruit?"

His eyes widened, and I chuckled. "Are they poisonous?" he asked.

I popped one in my mouth. "I think we'll live."

Laughing and rolling his eyes, he lowered himself to the ground, placing his interlocked hands under his head. "Remember when we were always here, Mae? Splashing and laughing while the older folk worried about the important things."

I settled on my side, keeping a respectable distance from his lean body. "I remember when Justinia used to come running down here to find you before your father realised you were missing from your studies—yet again."

Watching his lips stretch into a glorious smile, I

marvelled at the man my childhood friend had become. "What can I say? I don't have the same aptitude for learning as you."

"I think I have enough for the both of us." I knew this was an uncomfortable stretch of the truth. For some reason I was incapable of learning anything other than my herb lore. It was frustrating, and I didn't need Tristram teasing me about it.

Again, we lapsed into an easy silence, both of us staring at the grey morning sky.

"What's going to happen to us?" I asked, when the silence was too loud.

He rolled slightly, his swift gaze darting across my face and sweeping along the swell at the neckline of my dress. "To us? Well, one day I shall forgo my errant second son ways and make you my wife."

I batted him with my hand, ignoring the riotous stampede of wild herds in my chest. "Don't jest, Tristram. I mean us, our people?"

His gaze flickered with dark delving depths, but he stretched a grin on his face. "Oh that. Well, my father will return with his trusty and noble first born, who shall eventually bore us all into submission with his brooding brow."

Snorting, I clasped my hand over my mouth. "Tristram, you really don't take anything seriously, do you?"

His eyes shone with bright sparks of golden sunlight. "Some things I do." He rolled closer and edged his body next to mine. "I take you very seriously."

My cheeks burned a deep scorch. I shooed him away with my hands. I couldn't keep the dark cloud at bay though. "Truthfully though, Tristram. We are near to starving. The peace we keep with our neighbours is unsteady at best, and *now there are the new invaders creeping towards us. What hope do we have?"*

His eyes turned thoughtful as he watched me, his lips pursed. "We are a people not a place, Mae. We will move. Nothing we own can't be moved, or relocated, if we have to."

"Your father would never agree."

My thoughts skittered to my own father. Would he ever move away from the stones he was having brought here? Would he use his guidance and knowledge to move his people if it meant leaving his new temple behind? If I looked deep into my heart, I wasn't sure. "Things are changing. I can sense it."

Lifting his hand, he ran light fingertips along the edge of my face, sweeping across my skin. I held in my gasp, my heart skipping a beat. "Some things will never change."

"Promise?"

Our gazes locked. "Always."

A loud shout rose through the trees and he sighed. "I knew it would be too brief."

Impulsively I clutched at his hand—desperate to save the moment. "Be the man you want to be, Tristram, don't let others tell you the role you should fill."

Catching my hand, he lifted it to his mouth and planted a tender kiss on my palm. Unspoken words stalled between us, but the shouts became a cry. A sharp curse left his mouth as he rolled and jumped to his feet. "Something's wrong," he said.

My stomach chilled, as if it were held within an ice fist and I nodded. My attention was pulled by the river flowing at our feet. Bending, with no reasoning behind my actions, I pushed my hand into the cold waters. It flowed around my arm. The necklace at my throat warmed and thrummed.

"Mae, what are you doing?" Tristram stepped closer, but

for the first time in my existence he was at the very edge of my vision, not the centre.

A steeling strength ran from my hands along every limb of my body. I closed my lashes as an indescribable force pulsed deep with me. When I opened my eyes, it was as if my eyes were seeing for the first time. Every shaft of light, every blade of grass, every leaf on the trees, moved within my vision. I could have counted them all if I'd wanted.

My head whirled, and I stumbled, my body pitching for the water. Tristram's iron hard arm came around my stomach.

"Mae, what's wrong, are you ill?" His face was etched with worry, but all I could see was every tiny speck of his skin, every golden fibrous hair, every fleck of slate within his onyx eyes, even a faint birthmark I'd never noticed before. I could see everything. Everything.

"Something's changed." I gasped, drawing greedily at the morning air and my chest tightened and constricted. Using a control, I didn't know I possessed, I stopped myself from covering my eyes.

"What? Mae, talk to me. You're scaring me. You are in a swoon."

I shook my head and pushed away. His face crumpled momentarily with hurt. "I'm fine. Let's get back." How could I tell him I could suddenly see? That before the world had been drab and nondescript, but now it was alive with colour and sparkles. That the air moved and shifted every particle and individual element.

My fingers shook, and I reached for the secret birthing mark on his skin, my legs quivered, and I steeled myself up straight, holding my touch back from his face. My breath caught. I needed to speak to my father. Deep within the very centre of my being, I sensed a shift and change. Alarm bells set a warning off in my brain and I had to force myself not to run from Tristram. "Come, let's go back." I held one hand for his, willing the tremors to stop.

His gaze narrowed. The connection between us had never allowed for lies. Around us motes of lazy dust cascaded a waterfall of rainbow hues.

He spun as crashing footsteps fell through the trees nearest us. Hand on the hilt of the knife in his belt he pushed me behind him.

"It's okay, it's Alana and Deacon." The fall of my sister's footstep rang familiarly in my ear.

Tristram twisted a little towards me, his confused gaze meeting mine. "How do you know?"

How did I know? They weren't through the bushes yet. They crashed through moments after I announced their arrival. I shrugged at him, my eyes widening, but thankfully we didn't have the opportunity to discuss it.

Their faces made my stomach drop to my feet. My already shaking hands slicked with sweat. "Tristram, it's your father and Eernid."

"What? Are they home?" Tristram stepped forward, his face flooding with relief. His shoulders which had been tight and high for weeks relaxing. He let go of the knife in his belt, his hands swinging free.

"No." Deacon stepped up and clasped his hand on Tristram's shoulder. "They are dead."

Him and I, we stared at one another. Our faces the mirror image of shock. Everything froze around us, apart from within the depths of his gaze I watched a droplet of water form and disperse against his golden lashes. The only tear he would shed.

10

I watched Phil from across the history classroom. I'd forced myself to come back to school, to find the right class I was supposed to be in. It seemed ironic it was history. I struggled to stay awake, drifting in and out of daydreams and sleep—the unusually warm room wasn't helping. The heating in this place was messed up and my eyes kept falling closed. The dreams chased me and one minute I was in history, the next I was sitting with my feet in a river. Every so often I grabbed at the gem hidden under my white shirt. I was sure the ancient chain would break at any moment; I still couldn't believe I'd found it. I wanted to tell Phil that her parents were right, that there was something here, but we were separated by three rows of half-asleep students. My knee stung, and my kneecap ached with that soft tissue bruise that meant the pain never stopped.

I drummed my free hand on the desk in a bid to stay awake. I'd go for a run around the building if it meant not falling back to sleep and seeing where the dreams took me next. Seared in my memory, the vision of that single tear sparkling on *his* lashes was startlingly clear. The teacher scraped his chalk across the board and I coughed and tried to focus on the present.

Prince wasn't in history—for that I could only be grateful. Another round of 'do I want to run from him or to him' would have been exhausting.

"Nazi propaganda was essential to their war effort, why?" The teacher cast his spectacled gaze around the room and I slunk in my seat. I wasn't fast enough, and he settled on me. "Miss Adams, if I'm correct? Have you studied Nazi Germany before?"

Coughing, I straightened up, trying not to focus on any of the faces twisting in place to watch me squirm. "Not so much, we focused on the War of Independence."

The elderly teacher, his face wrinkled like scrunched paper, nodded understandingly. "Of course, you did." He stepped closer and I glared at him, willing him to let it go. "Using your highly intelligent brain, Miss Adams, which I am sure you have in there, what do you think propaganda could be used for by the Nazi's?"

With my skin heating to face-melting temperatures, I churned through my foggy brain. "To make people believe whatever they wanted, so not necessarily the truth."

He nodded slowly. "Yes, propaganda is highly manipulative, especially if it is used within the mechanism of state organised forms of media."

I nodded just to get him to go away. He smiled and waved at me with his hand. I assume he was telling me to relax. "I'm sure we can have a lively debate about the War of Independence between us, Miss Adams."

"Mm, great."

A snort filled the air and I shifted to see Phil in her seat with her face down towards her desk. The history teacher, whose name for the life of me I couldn't remember, glared first at Phil and then at me. I scrambled quickly—he was the history teacher, he might be able to help me find out about the stones. "I'd like that, we also did a lot about slavery and inequality."

He clapped his hands together. "Yes, yes, American history is rich in inequality."

I raised an eyebrow. "That's rich from a British person. Didn't you invent slavery?"

He laughed, a booming sound which made all the sleeping kids sit up straight. "Hahaha, yes they did. I on the other hand am Scottish, so am free from that English guilt."

He wandered back to the front of the classroom, snatching up his chalk and beginning to scratch it across the chalk board again, chuckling every so often to himself. I turned for Phil and glared at her, shaking my head. Holding her hands to the side she feigned innocence. I shook my head again and turned back for the front. The sooner this lesson was over, the quicker I could tell her what I found.

"Are you sure it was here?"
I stared bewildered at the shrubs and trees. "Yes, I'm sure." A sharp glance either way and I turn mystified for the path, waving my hand at the gravel I marched down only hours before. "He was—" I cut myself off. I didn't want to tell her I'd run into Tristan Prince again or explore the fact we inexplicably hated each other without reason. Nor the fact I couldn't stop thinking about him and maybe was dreaming about him in a freak out historical re-enactment.

Phil had the *hate to tell you, but you're totally crackers* look on her face. "Mum and Dad looked everywhere. The whole site was charted, graded, and searched. There was nothing, Mae, not even one speck of crockery, let alone standing stones."

On the rushed walk here I'd described the stones, trying to remember that place I knew existed somewhere in England, but whose name I couldn't recall. Stonehenge, apparently.

"I don't know if they were standing stones. They were smaller than pictures I've seen of Stonehenge."

She shrugged her shoulders. "There are different ones around the country, some smaller, some only partially surviving."

I shivered, even though the day had turned relatively dry. I say dry. What I meant was that the never ending wet whirling mist had lifted, but grey clouds still hung like dark curtains in the sky. "But the bones." I shook my head. The image of those tangled bones, the way the two skeletons seemed to be holding one another... it was unsettling. The image of them seemed to echo in my heart. "It was awful, Phil, they were huddled together. But how were they still there? Why haven't they been destroyed?" I went to tell her about the necklace, but reluctance stole my words. "Surely two skeletons can't remain intact like that, exposed to the elements?"

Phil shook her head. "No, they must be recent. Skeletons do survive, but they are buried in the earth. Locked in an unexpected pocket of soil which preserves them. If two skeletons had been left on stones out here in the wilderness, they would have been carried away a long time ago by wild animals."

I knew what she said was right, but I also knew she was wrong. I'd seen them. Felt them.

"I want to know everything." Out in the forest, alone, it should have been natural to feel uneasy. I didn't. I had no fear out here. I turned my view to the castle—I'd rather stay out here with the trees than go back in there with its draughty hallways and chilled bedrooms.

Phil shook her head again, this time with determination. "There isn't anything to find out."

I glared at the trees, sure they were teasing me, hiding my find so I couldn't share it with anyone else. "I reckon there's got to be records in this castle somewhere." I frowned at the sprawling crumbling reddish stone. "There has to be something, this place is too weird. Why is there a school in the middle of nowhere? Where is my aunt now? How does she find these artefacts you say she always sends back to the school?"

Phil and I stared at one another. My chest rose and fell with the agitated catch of my breath. "I know it's crazy, but I can sense something strange going on. I keep having these dreams, they are so real, exhausting even. Even in history I was having them." I glanced at where I thought the stones would be. It was as though I were stuck between times. Only half of me were here with Phil, the other half of me was... "It's this place." My voice was small, far away. "Can't you feel the pull of the trees? The air?"

Phil grabbed my hand. "Have you eaten today, Mae? You're freaking me out a bit, and you're very pale."

I pulled my hand away. "I'm fine. Just tired because I haven't slept properly since I got here. And I've probably lost a gallon of blood from this." I went to check on the wound across my knee, but there was nothing there. A trail of vine spread across my shoe, but there was no cut, no blood, no sore. *Shit.*

She frowned. "What am I looking at?"

"Nothing." My tongue was dry, my voice weak. I straightened but couldn't meet her eye.

"Mae," she carried on, "you haven't stopped sleeping since you got here."

I turned a grim expression for the trees. "There is something here, I know it."

Her fingers wound around my elbow. "Okay, I believe you. We can go searching, find out what we can. You are right, there are so many bits of this castle we don't have access to, anything could be here." She turned me back for the building. "I've always wondered why some of the outer wings are cordoned off. Maybe we can ask Mr Bonner if he knows? He likes you."

She was humouring me, but I appreciated it and I gave her fingers a squeeze. "Thanks. I promise I'm not crazy."

She laughed. "It's that room, I tell you."

I shivered and considered the prospect of room thirteen. The dreams were no longer just in room thirteen, though. Now they were everywhere. The memory of Tristan Prince and his sketch pad came back to me. Maybe I should tell Phil about that?

A shadow flickered under the low bough of a wide oak. A man, his shoulders broad, walked past, his hair glinting under the leaves. A leather belt slung around his hips, pinching a tunic in at his narrow waist. In his hand he held an axe. An axe I recognised.

I darted, chasing the shadow. The trees edged me along, so even when my breath became tight and laboured, I could still inhale the oxygen they supplied.

"Mae! Where are you going?" Phil's call was distant as I followed the shadow. I didn't stop.

It was him. Tristram. I could see him just as clear as I could feel him in my dreams.

· · ·

My crashing footsteps led me nowhere and eventually I staggered to a halt, hands on knees, breath screaming in my lungs. My legs quivered and buckled like a new born foal's and I crumpled to the ground. On my back and winded, I stared at the sky. It was darker, rolling with heavy clouds. It was going to rain again, *great.*

What was happening to me in this place? Clutching my head and running fingers through the tangled, strands of my hair, I tried to focus. Tried to see life with the logical cynicism I'd maintained through my entire unpredictable upbringing in New York. I wasn't stupid. You didn't survive the care system if you didn't have your wits about you. So why was I chasing fragments of dreams through the Scottish undergrowth?

Sighing, I lifted onto my elbows. I was losing my mind. It was official.

There they were. The stones. Tall and proud, two of them glinted, their speckled surface riddled with trails of moss and lichen were in touching distance. Scrambling to my knees, I moved towards them. Ivy and small buds of rose scattered around them like confetti. "Why won't you let anyone else see you?" My spoken words startled some birds, and I whirled around. The forest thrummed with life. Planting my hands onto the floor, I closed my eyes. My cynicism was truly switched off, dead and buried, as I felt into the ground.

Crazy but natural, all at once I stilled my mind and called to the earth. For a girl growing up in a cement jungle, my love of all things green had always been an unusual phenomenon. A warm tingle licked along my palm, and within my mind a shining vision of gold warmth spread until I sat basking in its glow as if on a summers day under the midday sun.

Move away. I told myself.

I ignored the prompt of reality and checked out of normal. "I don't want to move away."

Along my throat, my newly found gemstone vibrated and pulsed. I knew what I wanted. I wanted to see the shadow from my dream. *Him.* The haunting moments from my dreams chased me through the daylight hours, following and calling. Within me, somewhere deep in my soul I was desperate to dream so I could see him again.

The gem pulsed again, and I clutched it in my fingers. A thump echoed through the earth. It was agreeing with me. Opening my eyes, I blinked into sunlight. The warm glow I thought was in me, was just the sun peeking through the dense clouds.

My heart squeezed in my chest. What did I think? That I was like the girl from my dreams? I was nothing like her. The dreams were muddled: hazy, yet achingly real. They didn't make sense, but at the same time they were nothing but clear.

Impulsively, I scrambled to my knees, wading across the dry earth until I settled alongside the first stone. I pulled at the scrawled ivy, thorns from the wild roses stabbing the palms of my hands. "Ouch," One rigid thorn sent a gouge of blood along my lifeline. It oozed with crimson red and I stared at it in dismay. "That was unfair," I grumbled into the ethereal silence. My uninjured hand continued to uncover the grey slabs, running across the dimpled surface. My eyes stayed firmly averted from the embracing skeletons.

If my dreams were true—the memories of ghosts who lived before—then one of the huddled bundles of bones was the girl from my dream. The necklace now on my throat was hers.

I spun at the sound of a twig snapping behind me, finding only the trees waving their bent limbs at me. I reached for the stone, my bleeding, wounded hand scattered the debris and dirt, resting on the uneven surface.

Then I felt it. A deep rumble beneath my palm, a tingling pull running from my hand up my arm. Lifting onto both knees to reach better, I glided my hands over the stone as it vibrated under my touch. A low creak echoed like the opening of a door.

I wasn't dreaming. This was real.

Turning my hands over in amazement, I stared open mouthed at my clean palm. Not clean of dirt, but rather blood. The cut was gone. Peering closer at the stones I searched for any drop of blood but there was none, just the pitted surface of the ancient monument.

How had this stayed here unnoticed? Were these the stones I remembered from my muddled dreams, the ones being delivered, replacing the ancient oaks? My gaze travelled to the wide trunked sentinels. They barely seemed alive. Their branches were withered, their leaves absent.

With one hand still vibrating on the stone, I placed the other on the ground. The golden river of energy I'd mistaken for the sun warmed my limbs, running from one outstretched hand to the other.

"What's happening?" I whispered, my chest heaving with uncontrollable sobs. The earth wanted me. It was laughable, but I knew it to be true. Slipping off my shoes, I broke my connection with the ground to tug at my white ankle socks, discarding them on the ground. Then, using only my irrational instinct, I planted my feet back on the earth along with one hand, while my other slid back onto the stone which became increasingly familiar the more I touched it.

A shout blasted behind me and whirling from my bare footed position I turned to see if Phil had caught up with me and my mysterious stones. A girl with pale hair and a long dress pinched at the waist by a gilt belt ran past. My breathless exclamation caught in the air. I was asleep again.

Turning, I watched as she ran to an older man. His white robe swished across the floor as he stalked from a gathering of red-robed companions. "He's dead" the fair-haired girl cried.

I watched, almost as if a movie was on slow-mo, as the man with the white robe and matching hair reacted to her words.

"Alen?"

This was insane. There was no muddled fogginess about this dream. It was touchingly real.

"When?" The red-robed companions clustered around the girl, clamouring with questions and waving their hands to the cloud-filled sky.

"Their bodies have been returned. It wasn't the Druia; Ebrehered brought their bodies back over the border." The older man's face paled to the same shade as his hair and robes.

"It's the invaders. They come for our lands, our people." He glanced around, his bright-blue eyes ensnaring his audience. "Where is Mae?"

I crouched by the stone, but his eyes fell on me. "Mae, what are you doing there?" I looked behind me to see whom he talked to, but it was only the trees. My eyes narrowed. The trees. They'd changed, the brittle bark was replaced with a younger surface, the leaves a golden halo of bronze and rust.

"I'm not your Mae," I said, my voice croaking. His bright gaze, filled with confusion under a knotted brow, settled on my face as I managed to pull my hands from the stones.

I needed to wake up. Now.

"**M**ae!" The shout dragged my attention and I wiped at my brow. Sweat dripped into my eyelashes, stinging my eyes. Sweat, tears, it was all the same unwanted moisture.

"I'm here." I blinked into shadowed darkness and glared at the stones. They were again covered in ivy and spiteful roses, my efforts to clear them undone.

The trees wavered and shivered newly vibrant green leaves in my direction. Hadn't they been bare, the bark peeling and dying?

"Mae?"

I started in surprise at the male voice in the gloom. Assuming it was Jeffries out looking for me in the dark, I began to scramble up from the ground. Brushing at my legs, I remembered just as the shape loomed closer, that I'd taken my shoes and socks off.

I jumped, and my heart pounded in my throat. At first, I thought it was the shadow I'd chased out into the forest, but the tunic had been replaced by dark jeans and a navy t-shirt. Tristan Prince moved through the forest like a panther. I balled my fists, ready to fight the killer instinct I knew would rise within me at the sight of him. The gem against my skin heated until it scorched and sizzled. I grabbed it away, clutching it in my hands, expecting it to burn, but only finding it cool, and hard to the touch.

He stepped closer and my knees gave the most unaccountable shudder. "Mae, what are you doing out here? The whole school has been searching for you."

"I've only been out here for a while." It couldn't have been long since I ran away from Phil.

His face pinched with anxiety as he stepped closer. "No." His head shook from side to side and I watched mesmerised. My eyes wide, I could see him. Truly see him. Gorgeous, golden, and so handsome he'd make angels weep. "You've been gone for hours." His words rumbled with a deep vibration and my stomach flipped. A warm sensation heated the pit of my belly.

"Wha—" surprised I was even talking to him, I was even more surprised when he interrupted me.

"It's the strangest thing."

"What?" My tongue dried.

He stood in the shadow, but his face was alive with emotion. His eyes swept over me from the top of my head to the soles of my bare feet. Not a single inch of my body missed his appraising evaluation. His lips curved at the edges as if he liked what he saw—it would have been rude and worth me giving him hell for if I wasn't also doing the same. My own gaze greedily absorbed every inch of him. It was like living in the dark and then someone switching the light on.

"I don't want to kill you." He shuddered a sigh of relief. "Thank fuck for that." His black gaze warmed, and he stepped a little closer. "I was dreading being the one to find you in case I ended up burying you out here in the woods," he hesitated. "But, now I'm glad I did." A frown flickered across his brow. "I would have been mad if anyone else had." He seemed puzzled, which was about right, because I was beyond confused. "Strange." His deep honey voice made my bones ache. Now he was talking, it was as if I'd always known his voice.

A ridiculous faint smile flitted on my lips. "That's a relief. I'd like not to be buried out here." Was I making small talk with the guy now? About him killing me and burying my body in the woods of all things? I'd be checking myself in for psychiatric help at this rate.

He dropped his dark gaze to my bare feet in the dirt. "I'm sorry about last night. I don't know what came over me." When he met my eyes, my breath became heavy and dense, like the air before a thunderstorm.

Still clutched in my now sweaty palm the gem pulsed one solid thrum like a heartbeat.

"It's okay, I would have done the same." I hesitated. "Although it seems odd now." We both paused. Only a metre or so separated us and we stood there with our hands hanging at our sides, two total strangers having the most erratic conversation.

His lips stretched into a small smile and the dark depths of his eyes lighted for a brief moment. "Are you injured?"

"Pardon?"

He nodded towards my feet, my toes dirty and scratched. "No, uh —" I had nothing to say that wasn't all levels of intense craziness. "Have I really been gone for hours?"

He nodded when he met my gaze. His smile stretched into a grin. "Philomena Potts has been running around telling everyone her best friend has been stolen by ghosts."

I groaned and palmed a sticky hand through my hair. "Great."

Now I was the new girl in the centre of a drama—wasn't the first time.

Was I the new girl... wasn't I leaving...?

He coughed and pushed his hands into his jeans. "I should get you back." God, his voice. It did something crazy to my insides.

"Yeah, hold on. I'll put my shoes on."

"No need. Here." I shrieked like a girly girl as he swept me up into his arms and then folded his legs to grab my shoes.

"I'm fine, I can walk." I struggled, but he pinned me tight against his broad chest. The scent clinging to his t-shirt was divine: herbs and fresh air. I could have gone for a full swoon if I hadn't been burning with embarrassment at being carried like a child.

"We will get there quicker if we go my way."

"How do you know the way through the forest?" The hairs on my arms stood on end.

My question was met by a brief beat of silence. "I don't know." He shrugged, and it jostled me against his chest. The gem pulsed again. "I just do."

As silly as I felt being carried when there was nothing wrong with me, I relaxed in his hold. When we got back to school, he dropped me with little ceremony onto my bare feet. "Thanks for finding me," I called after his retreating form as he slipped into the shadows. He didn't stop, nor did he answer. Tristan Prince was gone again.

11

Caledonia

I t had been a day since everything had changed.

Tristram sat huddled with my father as they knelt by the mutilated body of his father. Together they were asking the gods to guide Alen and Eernid into the next life.

Today they would be buried with the honour they deserved.

What had happened nobody knew. The Druria from the bordering lands insisted on their innocence. The rumour of the invaders foreign to this isle ran around the settlement, until mothers were keeping their children inside and the men wore pinched, tight expressions on their faces as they patrolled the circular wall around our homes.

Times had changed. In one cycle of the sun and moon I knew they'd changed forever. How I knew I couldn't explain. While Tristram had been locked away with Father and the high priests of our order I'd felt a shift within me. The gem Heather had given me felt hot against my skin. I grabbed it now, holding it until my hand was warm as if it had been toasted next to the central hearth.

It seemed childish but in my naïve hopefulness I'd hoped the gem would help me find a way to be who I needed to be, and to be with Tristram. Now I realise that futile hope had been just that—a misplaced hope. The gem was connecting me to something else. What that was I couldn't explain.

I watched from my spot on a stool by the front of the round house. Clerics worked the land around me, tending to my herbs as I sat and waited. Waited for what, I didn't know.

Tristram's face was shallow, his eyes sunken. The light golden flare with which he lit our small society was snuffed out. I stared at him, willing him to catch my eye, but he didn't look in my direction, although surely he must have known I was there. My red cloak was hardly unmistakable.

Finally, when all of me—excluding my still warm hand —had frozen in the morning chill, they rose from their prayers. I scuttled off the stool, pushing it back, scaring a chicken pecking around my feet.

"Tristram." My feet stomped, leaden, as I walked towards my friend. My hand reached for him but hesitated when flat black eyes met mine. "Tristram, how goes you?" It was a stupid question.

His face remained blank, his gaze unknowing at my greeting. He straightened his back, coming out of his dream. "I am fine, My Baduri."

Why wouldn't he meet my gaze? Hadn't it been yesterday we'd laid by the river as close as two people could be? Father frowned in my direction but then turned with a swirl of his cloak and went to organise some priests clustered and waiting for instruction.

"Tristram," I ran a gentle hand along his forearm, but he pulled his skin out from under my touch. "Please talk to me.

What have you and father spoken about? What are we going to do?"

His lips settled into a firm line, his eyelids dropping into slits. "We shall bury my father and then I will be named leader. It's the will of the priest."

My heart hammered. Tristram wasn't the man who was supposed to lead us. This was a terrible mistake. He was the man who was meant to maintain our status quo, to keep us happy in our miserable winter months, to care about us all.

A leader had to be too ruthless. A leader had to lead without thought.

"Tristram, I'm worried for you."

His top lip lifted, and he huffed a breath through his nose. "You think I'm not the man to lead us?"

My mouth fell open. "No." I stuttered though, and his black filled gaze burned. "I think you are every man, but my father, he is distracted at the moment. I don't know if he can guide you."

"And will you? Guide me if I need it?"

I bowed my head. This was no longer my Tristram in front of me. He was my leader. "If you request it, My Lord."

My words hurt, they caught in my throat and made me wince.

"I do. I suggest you finish your training, Baduri. We will have a long fight against these invaders."

"Fight?" My hands reached for him but froze mid-air. "The foreigners will tear us apart. They want our land and resources. No invader has ever come to these shores in peace."

"And you know this because you are fluent in our lore and histories?" He raised a fair eyebrow, his dark eyes sweeping across my face; no warmth I would expect in a curve of his lips.

"Yes." My mind freed itself, spinning and stretching, filling itself with a visual picture. As if I'd written the past myself, the image came to me. "The red-haired warriors came from over the sea, their chariots spinning in the earth, taking all the land they could, stealing our women and livestock."

Tristram's face dropped. "You hate histories."

He wasn't wrong. In fact, he was incredibly right.

The image inside my mind, grew and expanded until it was all I could see. "They stayed, became our neighbours, accepted our ways." I thought of Ebrehered of the neighbouring clan. His hair a pale copper, wild and tangled, his skin covered in smatterings of darkened dots. Then I saw a swirl of red, splashes of vibrant colour, glimmering with gold as bright as the sun, sweeping across our drab and dour land.

I'd never met Ebrehered before. I didn't know from where his people had come. But I knew now without any doubt his ancestors had landed on our shores, dressed in deer skins, and explored our wild terrain. It was a baduri, like myself, who had tamed the wild men and made them put down the roots of their settlement.

My eyes flew open and my shaking fingers fell against my lips before I could say anything else.

Turning on my heel I launched myself to run into the forest.

"Baduri, you must stay within the settlement." Tristram's hot hand curled around my arm with an easy grip.

"Remove your hands from my arm." I glared at the stranger before me. How dare he call me his priestess. How dare he speak to me in that way, when I'd always been so much more to him.

Furious, I launched my hands against his chest, pushing him back. "Stay away from me, Tristram." Gathering the skirts of my cotton dress in my shaking hands I prepared to run.

"Mae, wait."

I hesitated, his voice darting through my stomach like an arrow attached to finely spun string. The gem against my throat heated and pulsed. When I turned, his face was torn, his fair eyebrows knotted together, his lower lips drawn between his teeth. "You will come to the burial with me, Mae?"

I could sense the annoyance in the question. Before yesterday I would never have not gone with him.

I dropped a curtsey and his frown deepened. "As you wish, My Lord."

And then I ran, far away from Tristram, far away from our devastated people. But the images of the past, the stories I hadn't yet learned, stayed in my head no matter how fast I ran.

I t was Heather who found me with my toes dipped into the clear cool run of the river. It wasn't the same as the day before. I wished I could erase time, wished that yesterday had never taken place, that I hadn't turned eighteen. Same as I wished Alen hadn't marched out to meet the invaders without waiting and pausing for thought first. Out of all the things I wished for, being able to remember Tristram's hardened gaze was the one I wanted to change the most. He was twenty—we'd spent uneasy years living in peace with our neighbours, the rhythm of our lives settling into a comfortable ebb. He shouldn't be the man who led us to our end. He deserved more.

"What are you thinking?" Heather settled beside me, her

bracelets clacking. She frowned at the water as it swirled around my toes.

I turned to her, shielding my face from a beam of sunlight slanting through the boughs of a young oak. "I was wishing the water could wash everything away: every hurt, every tear, every argument."

Heather smiled and patted my hand. "Water can do many things. I'm not sure it can erase the past."

I splashed my feet, sending droplets of shimmering water flying. "What can it do?"

"Ask it." She shrugged, and I groaned.

"Are we going to talk in riddles again? I'm tired, I didn't sleep." I didn't want to tell her about the muddled dark dreams. I was unable to make sense of them, but it was as though I were being called but I didn't know how to answer.

Her lips tipped up in a sad smile. "Of course, you didn't sleep. Yesterday was a big day."

"Everything changed," I grumbled, "And not for the better."

She shrugged again. "Everything changed for you." She peered at the neckline of my dress. "And the gem, you've been wearing it?"

Lifting a hand, I slipped it out from where it was hidden under the dark wool of my clothes. "Yes, although it's strange; sometimes it feels hot, others cool."

"It's coaxing the magic out of you, unlocking your skills."

I stared at her. Then I stared some more, ready to see her gap-toothed grin as she smacked the floor at her hilarity. She didn't.

"I don't have magic. Magic is given by the gods to a select few. No bard has seen real magic in our lifetime."

Although bards and baduri's were trained in the law of old and could appeal to the gods, some of us—my father was one— could influence the weather sometimes, although even that skill seemed to be slipping. But we hadn't seen real magic, the type that flowed through the earth, for a long time, although each settlement, each tribe, liked to maintain they were the ones with the old skill. It kept the neighbouring clans in line. No one liked the prospect of fire and brimstone coming down.

How did I know this?

My eyes widened, and I stared at Heather.

I hadn't bothered to listen to the early law. Forgotten laws and skills bored me. I wanted to know about herbs; real talents I could learn and help people with. It was why Father despaired of me ever finishing my training.

"Heather, something is happening to me."

She grinned and there was the toothless smile I'd been expecting. "Embrace it."

"I don't know what it is." My skin prickled, my hair standing on end.

"Neither do I, but I've always sensed it in you. Since you were a babe landing in my hands."

"Sensed what?" I wanted to pull my feet from the water. The gentle waves lapped around my ankles in silken pulses and as crazy as it sounded it was as if the water was listening to our conversation.

"Something old."

My mouth dried until my tongue tingled. "What do you mean old?"

She shrugged which was becoming increasingly annoy- ing. "Old as the hills, as old as the water, maybe even as old as the air we breathe in here." She tapped beneath my chest, beneath the pendant.

"Me?" I pushed my hair back, trying to regulate my haggard breathing. "Me?"

"You." Her eyes twinkled.

"But you're the magical one: always disappearing, always managing to guide babies so successfully into our world." I glanced at the world we brought them into. Swaying trees, green and brown. The shimmer of crystal clear water... and then the threat of attack... death.

"I'm no more magical than those trees."

I frowned at our sacred grove. Out of sight were the ghastly stones Father was rolling in.

"But—"

She cut me off. "I'm a conduit. I feel energy. Sometimes I feel the old ways, sometimes the new." She quizzed me with an appraising glance. "Sometimes the unknown."

A conduit? What in the name of the gods was that? "Does my father know?"

Her smile transformed into a smirk. "Your father doesn't know everything." Her smile faltered at the edges, the deep wrinkles in her face transforming into soft creases. "And he's on a dangerous path, misguided, like a fool searching for riches where they can't be found."

She was only telling me what my soul had already hinted at. Father and those stones; it was a dark path into his future he was walking.

"And this necklace?" I lifted the now cool gem into my hand. It only warmed when Tristan was near. "What's this for?"

"It's not just for this life." Her wrinkles creased until she resembled the bark of the nearby trees. "It's to guide you in the others. To help you connect—to help you remember."

"What do you mean?"

Heather closed her eyes. This wasn't the time to go to

sleep. I wanted to know more. Wanted to know what she meant.

"Mae, there you are." I jumped and my feet splashed out of the water. Alana moved through the shadows of the forest glade, her dark dress blending with the murky canopy of the trees, making her pale-silver hair stand out in vibrant contrast. She stared at me, her face crinkled. "What are you doing out here? The burial is waiting to start. Father says you must come."

I turned to Heather, as if my sitting next to her was answer enough, but again the lady was gone. My skin prickled. "I was..." I lost my words. I was what? Talking to a ghost? Someone who I wasn't sure actually existed? How else could I explain the mysterious comings and goings of the Kneel Woman. "I don't know if I can come."

Alana frowned and settled next to me on the riverbank. "Why? Alen was our leader. It is proper and right we show him full respect on his passing to his next life."

I fingered the gem at my throat. The next life. What if this gem was meant to do something for the next life like Heather had said? I wished she didn't talk in riddles as much as she did.

Alana's shoulder nudged my gently. "Mae, Tristram needs you."

"Does he? He doesn't seem to like me very much right now."

She smiled, a small sad flirting curl of her lips. "Tristram will always like you above any other. I don't know what it is about the two of you, but you seem tied together in your friendship."

I snorted low. "I don't think the new leader of our clan wants to be friends."

"He's hurting, Mae. This isn't what he expected."

"Yeah, well maybe I'm hurting too."

I thought of the new sensations running in my veins. The images, the knowledge, the memories I knew couldn't belong to me. I opened my mouth to tell Alana, to share my burden with my dear sister, but the words halted on my lips at the loud blast of a horn. I'd know that sound anywhere. My stomach pinched and twisted.

Was I going to leave Tristram to face this alone, while the rest of our people watched his every move?

Silently, I rose to my feet. My toes still tingled from the cool water and I looked longingly at the crystal current. I'll be back to learn more, I told it. Then I held my hand for Alana and led us back towards the settlement.

Man, woman, and child, stood in a silent circle, Father in the middle, his arms risen to the sky as he chanted and prayed to our gods to lead Alen on into his next life.

Reincarnation was the root of all existence, our souls only tied to the mortal plane through the skin and bones of our bodies. Strength was to be found in death. Another doorway into a different life.

I slipped through the crowd of silent onlookers. Father was murmuring the rites of passage, calling on Lugh the god of rebirth. My hand found Tristram's, winding my fingers with his, the gem on my neck heating at our touch. I glanced up at him to find his face forward, his lips grim, his eyes burning dark. He didn't turn to me, but his hand squeezed mine.

While everyone worshiped the god of rebirth and sought Alen a safe journey, my thoughts drifted and I watched the clear sky. From under my feet the earth pulsed, and I glanced around to see if anyone else felt it. Nobody moved.

Surrounded by my people, my hand in the man I'd always loved's, I slipped into an isolation of unfathomed depths.

Who was I? And why was this happening?

I thought of rebirth, my eyes flicking to Tristram. Could I imagine a life where he wasn't in it? But yet, didn't that always happen? Why should I be different?

With a multitude of unanswerable thoughts and questions swirling in my head and a thunderous gathering of rain clouds swirling above, I reached into the air, seeking answers from wherever I may find them.

What was magic? And if the magic of old, long disappeared had come back, why had it come to me?

An eagle swirled overhead, wheeling and squawking in a bank of wind. From under its wings I could make out the glimmer of a second pair of wings. Iridescent and breathtaking, they stretched in a shimmering rainbow of lights.

The eagle's head turned, his beady black eyes meeting mine, and I gave him a nod as he banked higher into the azure of the sky, taking his stunning soul with him. The time of Alen had passed.

L ater, with the freshly dug mound of earth still settling into a new page of our history, Father lead Tristram out to his new stones. There my childhood friend was named our leader and liege. All knelt before him as Father placed upon his head a circlet of copper and crystal.

My heart pounded heavy and the earth rumbled under my feet.

Times were changing but was I ready for the change they were bringing?

12

"So let me get this straight." Phil stared at me from across the table. I'd been scolded by the sharpened tongue of Mrs Cox for running off into the forest, told it was dangerous to leave myself exposed in the wild like that. Then I'd been given a hot cocoa and a plate of cabbage and mash potato. Unwanted glances lingered in my direction. The whole school knew of my excursion and whispers crept around the cavernous space. And to think I'd wanted to avoid drama.

I clattered my cutlery as I put them down and pushed my plate away. How could I eat when I wasn't sure what I'd just experienced? More to the point how much boiled cabbage was I supposed to eat anyway?

Phil was intent on my story, her glasses repeatedly slipping down her nose as she stared at me. "You found the stones, and they..." she trailed off and I didn't blame her. My story was one of fantasy, the misgivings of an overactive imagination. Except I'd felt it all. Brief as it had been, I'd sat by those stones when the trees were younger and the people around me weren't wearing a navy uniform.

"Phil." I leant forward dropping my voice. "Something's going on here. I've been feeling it since I arrived." I wanted to grab her hand, to squeeze it tight, so she'd listen more, but I'd had enough people talk about me for the day. "These dreams I've been having, they are so real, but then when I wake it's as if they are being hidden from me."

She nodded, her face blank.

"What if I'm not dreaming? What if it's happening?"

Licking her lips, I watched her dig deep for a suitable response. "So somewhere there are a bunch of Druids just running around and no one else can see them apart from you?" She pushed her glasses up again, her eyes beneath the lenses crinkled with concern.

I shook my head. That didn't sound right. "No." I sighed. "I don't know what I mean." I hesitated for a moment before throwing caution to the wind and revealing my true crazy. "Tristan, he's in my dreams, but he's different, he's—"

"Ah," she shouted. "Now that I can explain." She waved her fork in my direction. "We've all dreamed of Tristan Prince, and who can blame us, the guy is a god of extreme hotness."

I was going to retort, tell her that no one could possibly have dreamed of the Tristan I dreamed of. A stab of jealousy quickened my pulse. I didn't want to share Tristan, dream or not.

"Can I sit?"

Phil's face fell and then turned a vibrant shade of purple as we both silently watched Tristan Prince pull out the chair opposite mine.

"Bleugh, bah bleugh." Phil's lips moved but she lost all control of the English language.

Was he for real? Was he going to sit at our table and

watch us eat cabbage? My stomach twisted into knots in flat refusal. I glanced at his own tray; it only contained a bottle of water.

My heart began to palpitate until I thought I might hurl. I didn't want to kill him anymore, but my body responded like a lit match to his closeness.

Phil's mouth hung open.

His dark gaze settled on my face when he spoke, his voice warm drops of honey. Low and melodic. "I wanted to check you were okay." He grabbed at the bottle of water, but then left it where it was.

"I'm..." My brain forgot every word I'd ever spoken. "I'm..." Nope. Honestly, I had nothing of any use between my ears.

"She's fine, absolutely fine," Phil assured him. "Good job you found her though. She could have been eaten by wolves, attacked by highland gypsies. All sorts."

I tried to kick her under the table but jabbed his shin instead. Officially that was the last time I was going to attempt a subtle 'shut the hell up'.

His dark gaze flitted over her and that stab of jealousy flowed into an outright wave of agitation. "I didn't know there were many wolves left in these parts."

She nodded. "Oh yes, when my folks were here doing their research they found loads of evidence of wild packs." Her cheeks scorched. "And that's me geeking out." She stared at me intently. "Although, Mae is into history, aren't you, Mae?"

I glared at her. "Sometimes."

"She was just telling me about these weird dreams she's been having." This time my foot connected with the right shin and she squealed, pulling her lips tight into a grimace.

Tristan eyes zoned in on me like a search light.

Thoughtfully they ran over my face, absorbing my hair, my eyes... my mouth. "This place has that effect." He twisted the plastic cap on his bottle and I watched, mesmerised, as he took a long sip. Phil was almost panting, her tongue lolling like a retriever chasing a ball.

"How long have you been here?" Phil asked, feigning a crooked innocence. Like she didn't damn well know. She knew everything.

His lips hinted at a smile, his gaze still focused on my face until he graced Phil with a light nod. "I thought you knew everything, Philomena Potts."

Phil squeaked. She actually squeaked. Before she had a chance to reply he snapped his attention back on my face, staring at me intently. Silently, we watched one another. Staring in mute mode was better than attempting to strangle one another. Although my heart still raced like I was stuck in fight or flight mode.

"So, any gossip from the boy's side?" Phil asked, leaning her head into her hand.

"No." He didn't take his eyes off me.

"I heard Luke Simmons was going to ask Charlie to hang during social tomorrow."

Her words pulled me out of my reverie. "Social?" I tore my eyes from Tristan's face and turned to my Phil. "What social?"

She groaned, and Tristan fiddled with his bottle top, spinning it on the table. "Well, you know like I said we aren't allowed in each other's quarters? Once a week we have a social mixer, organised by Mrs Cox. It's horrific on every level from here down to hell. We will watch a terrible historical movie and then be given a quiz on it after."

"That does sound like hell." I smiled. There was no way on earth I was going to that. Not ever.

She smirked. "You are so coming. It's compulsory."

I shook my head. "Nope, I've had a traumatic experience today getting lost in the forest, I'll be let off."

She laughed while Tristan sat there leaning back in his chair, his long legs stretched out, silently watching us. How did he manage to make the uniform look cool? I felt like a prize idiot in mine. "I don't think so. Mrs Cox is *very* enthusiastic about the social mixer."

I shrugged. Whatever, it wasn't a big deal. I had other things on my mind. My eyes wandered back towards Tristan like a moth to a flame. "You saw the stones I was sat by, didn't you?" I wavered a little. What if he hadn't seen them? What if I was really crazy? The necklace on my neck warmed and vibrated.

I clutched it in my hand and Tristan's face dropped as he saw it. *Did he recognise it?*

My pulse thudded loudly in my ears and the room began to tilt at a strange angle. "Mae!" Phil called, but it was like hearing her through water. Once when I'd been ten my foster mum at the time had taken me swimming. I'd gone too deep and she was calling me to come back, but I'd been unable to lift my head to hear her properly. The memory held me fast. How had I got my head above the water? Closing my eyes, the thudding still pounding in my ears like an out of time drum. I recalled that day. The pool... it had been crowded... I'd always thought a guard had caught me and lifted me up. But there had been no hands. No lift. I'd just surged on the side like a fish flapping on a bank.

"I think I'm going to be sick." I muttered. But if I was talking in the past, staring at the face of a woman from my childhood, or talking to Phil I didn't know.

Cool hands smoothed my face. "Mae?" and I blinked into deep pools of liquid ink. His face was at once recognisable, not just from my dreams, but from somewhere deep within me. "I know you." The room faded around me, but I carried on staring at his eyes.

It was clear. Crystal. The face of the boy who yesterday I'd wanted to slash with a carving knife was one I knew with as much familiarity as I knew my own.

"And I know you." His lips curved at the edges deliciously sweet.

"This is all hunky dory," Phil's voice cut through the static in my head, but it was too late, my grip on reality started to slip.

W hen I came to, the chill in the room was so extreme I wiggled my nose to make sure it was still there. It was, but frozen like an ice block. I rubbed at it, wondering if I'd succumb to frostbite staying in room thirteen.

"It's bloody freezing in here." I jumped at the deep rumble.

"Tristram?" Sleep fuddled my lucidity. The Tristram I'd just been with had been cold and aloof, my feelings burned by his distance.

My feelings?

Scurrying back against my mattress, I sat up and gathered the blankets around me to keep warm. The room was dark, shadowed, and deep, lit only by the faintest glimmer through the leaded window.

I gasped as firm fingers slid around my wrist, holding my fragile bones tightly. A tug dragged me closer to his shadowy form. My mouth tingled with drying anxiety. "You're keeping secrets from me?"

"What?" I tried to pull away, but he held me firm.

Shifting in the dark, his face slowly took shape, hardened and firm, his eyes were focused anywhere apart from at me.

"Mae, I know you better than anyone, better than you know yourself. You are lying to your liege."

I scurried back, my spine hitting the wall as his lips hesitated over mine. "Tristan, stop, you're scaring me."

"I could have any woman, Mae. Any of them would beg to be my wife, to have me as their lover."

My stomach twisted at his words, that flood of jealousy stealing back over my rationality.

"But not you." He laughed a harsh burst of bitter mirth. "Not you." His nose skimmed my cheek, and I held my breath. A heady rush of soap and forest air swirled through my senses. "I want you though, I've never wanted anything more."

My hands tore free from his grasp and I shoved his chest. "Tristan." He didn't move, his thoughts far away.

"Tristan. Stop it." A sob tore from my mouth.

His eyes blinked onto mine. Liquid obsidian pools I could have happily drowned in. "Mae?" Rubbing his face, he blinked. "I was sleeping. I dozed off waiting for you to wake."

"Why are you here?" I couldn't calm the thrashing jangle of my nerves. Free of his hold I rolled from the bed and backed into the wall.

"I had to check you were okay." He hung his head. "I didn't want to hurt you again. I promise."

"You're having the dreams too, aren't you? The dreams I've been having."

His eyes met mine and my legs quaked, my knees knocking together. "Yes."

"What are you dreaming?" I wanted to know it was the same, that I wasn't crazy.

"About you." He looked down, bashing the toe of his trainer. His fingers flexed and tightened into fists before releasing again. I wasn't scared though. It was another sensation moving inside me.

"Me? You can't be." I wanted to keep my sanity, even though I was fast free diving off the cliff of normality. "We don't know one another. We hate each other. How can we be dreaming about each other...?" I ran out of words. We had hated one another and then I'd found that necklace and the next thing we were sitting exchanging pleasantries at lunch. I clutched my head—nothing made sense. Nothing.

He looked like the man from my dreams, there was no denying it, but I wouldn't say it was him. *Would I?* I stared closer and then closed my eyes, remembering the scent of forest that clung to him as he moved near me.

I could explain that though. He'd found me in the forest only hours before. An erratic snort presented itself as a laugh. *Hours?* I didn't have a clue what the time was. I'd done nothing but sleep in this cursed place.

Curse.

The word bolted out of the blue.

Curse.

What if Tristan and I were cursed? How else could you explain the way we'd hated one another on sight?

But why would we be? I was a Yank, this the first time my feet were on foreign soil. He was British with a serious stick of arrogance shoved up his ass.

Unless.

Unless.

I couldn't. I couldn't go there.

I clutched at the gem, pulling the chain free from my clothes. His eyes landed on it and I knew he recognised it. "We only stopped hating each other when I found this."

He was across the room, crowding into my space. "Where did you find that?"

"On the bones, I found it on the stones." My voice wavered.

"Mae." My name was the lightest of whispers.

I closed my eyes and his breath fanned across my face. With a shaking gulp of air, I considered the possibility all of this was real. That we were living the dreams of those who'd walked before us.

Had I always been destined to be here? My parents' car crash? Was that a spin of the wheel of fortune that made the letter from my aunt a necessity?

And why had Tristram and I found each other now? Was this the first time since the life in the forest—the life that seemingly ended on those stones?

With my eyes still closed I considered all the many variations of crazy that were possible.

The kiss took me by surprise and I gasped as his lips skimmed mine. The faintest touch, the tickle of butterfly wings. A fire sparked and lit within me. I grabbed at his face with my hands, anchoring his lips to mine. His body pressed mine against the stone wall. We were the fire held up by the stones. The more I kissed his lips: firm and supple, his tongue teasing and darting, the more I needed him as much as I needed air to breathe.

The kiss was all consuming. I groaned as his body pressed against mine. Rigid and hard, he pushed against the softness of my curves. Desire ran through my body as deep as all the rivers of the world pouring together into the sea.

When he broke the kiss, and he rested his forehead against mine, it was if I'd been sliced in half. I gasped and attempted, without much success, to settle my breath. "What's going on, Tristan? I don't understand any of this."

A slow smile tilted his lips. "I don't know, My Baduri, but I believe we are together for a reason."

"I'm not her, Tristan." It was stupid talking about a girl from a dream as if she were real. "I'm not a priestess. I don't have magic."

His eyes settled on my face. "Yet."

I laughed and whirled away. "You really believe all this? You believe we are them? It's not possible."

His eyes flashed. "Didn't people believe in reincarnation?"

He said the word. He actually said the word. My heart hammered. "You're crazy."

The lids of his eyes dropped to hooded lust-filled pockets. "Maybe."

"I've got to get out of this place, it's making me insane. I'm calling a cab and going straight back to the airport." I didn't know how I'd call a cab, or how I'd pay for it, let alone the flight I'd take to whisk me home to the world of sanity —Queens.

His hand snaked around my waist, pulling me closer. My traitorous body melted a little as I gazed into his golden face. "We've found one another, Mae. I know you. Even when I wanted to kill you I knew you. The reaction we had to one another—strangers don't have that. It's logical we know one another, are fond of one another." His voice dropped a notch and my tummy flipped.

I shook my head. "No. I can't believe it."

A flash of annoyance flitted across his features. "Here, come and see this."

Tight fingers gripped my hand and he yanked on the door, pulling me out into the dark hallway. It was late, no sounds drifted from behind closed doors.

We walked through hallways I hadn't yet found, which

was ironic considering I thought I'd been lost down most of them. Finally, he pushed through a different door. I started at the number on the wood. Thirteen.

Inside, the room was plastered with pieces of white paper. Silently, I stepped forward while he waited and watched at the door. The papers all held images of me.

"What is this?"

He followed me in, the door closing softly behind him. The flicker of desire rekindled in my stomach although I tried to extinguish it before it could take hold. Leaning down he grabbed a sketch pad off the bed and waved it at me. "These are the ones I've drawn this week." He pointed to the walls. "These are the ones I drew before you arrived."

I was silent. Mute with surprise.

He turned and grabbed for his wallet, yanking a folded, aged piece of paper from a bundle of receipt bills. "And this is the sketch I drew when I was ten and my mother bought me my first set of charcoals."

My hands shook as I took the tattered scrap of paper. My face stared back at me, red waves and large grey eyes.

"How?" my legs wobbled close to collapse.

"I don't know," he murmured. I continued to stare at the paper until he tilted my chin with gentle fingers. "But I'm willing to find out if you are."

I stared at him. Speechless.

"Mae, I feel like I know you." His fingers caught mine and he pressed my hand against his chest. "Here."

I nodded. I didn't know what I thought or felt. I didn't know anything of any use to anyone. But I knew what had been happening to me since I'd arrived here, and I knew the gem on my neck scorched my skin as he touched me.

"But the dreams. They are facing the Romans. Something was coming to change their lives. Why have we found each other now? What happened to them, Tristan? How did they end up on those stones?" My words caught in my throat, tied up in a sob. "How did they end up tangled together, left for me to find?"

His eyes held mine and I drowned in their dark liquid depths. "I don't know, but we can find out—together."

I nodded.

I didn't have anything left. But I knew I wouldn't leave the room without him. In my soul, in a piece of me I never knew existed, like the rainbow iridescent wings floating under that eagle in my dream, I knew I'd found him. And I knew now I had, anything was possible.

"I don't want to go back to my room." I looked up at him through my lashes.

"Stay."

13

Caledonia

"**F**ather, have you seen Heather?" I tried to capture his attention quickly before I lost him again. His frequent wandering was becoming rifer. My hands soothed the scalp of the boy in front of me. His skin seethed with sores, festering scabs he kept scratching and causing to bleed. "Aeneid, are you still scratching these?" I bent my knees, so I could meet the refugee's eyes. He nibbled his lips and shook his head and I gave him a rueful smile.

"You can't fib to me, little one, I know everything." I kept one eye on Father making sure he didn't escape before I could pin him down. I hadn't seen Heather since the river and I needed to ask her questions; more questions than I knew the words for.

"I'm not lying, Priestess." The little scrap shook when he realised he'd called me by my title and not Mae as I'd asked him to do at least twenty times in the last few days.

I smiled and pulled his scrawny shoulders into my arms for a swift hug. "Many wouldn't believe you, Aeneid, but I will." I grinned. "Just this once." He relaxed under my touch and I frowned as I cast him over with critical assessment. The number of drifting refugees we'd had entering our lands the last week was increasing. The little boy in front of me had no one and he couldn't, or wouldn't, tell us what he'd witnessed.

"I'll use my balm one more time and then you should be healed." I frowned at his scalp. Now who was lying?

Reaching into the wooden bowl of water next to me on the stool I swirled the seeping herbs, releasing the pungent scent of spruce and nettle. The sores needed a deep clean before I anointed them with a cream I'd churned from animal fat and herbs. The water ran around my fingers. Since my time at the river with Heather the day of the burial, my experience of water was greatly changed. Before, as I felt was the norm, water was a substance you could easily pull one's hand through. It moved for you. Now, the water fought against me. Even in a still bowl carved from simple wood I could sense the strength of the converged droplets beneath my touch.

Scooping a palmful of the glistening liquid, I smoothed it over Aeneid's matted, scab filled, hair.

Wouldn't it be wonderful if the water could heal him?

I blinked at the ridiculous thought. Water didn't heal. Not directly. It cleansed, purified, created a space in which healing could take place.

"Eran following." I frowned at the unwarranted words which tumbled out of my mouth.

"What did you say, Prie—Mae?"

I coughed. "Nothing." I shook my head and forced a smile, dipping my head as my cheeks blushed.

"Eran following." This time I gasped as the strange words bubbled to my lips. My hand held Aeneid's head, my *thumb soothing the strands of hair. My palm tingled with a sharp itch.*

"Oh," I exclaimed, turning my hand over to inspect for a bite. He must have bugs in his hair for me to get bitten like that. In alarm, I looked at my palm, finding it covered in dried scabs. I rubbed at them, sweat beading along the back of my neck as a steady panic elevated my heartbeat to that of an escaping deer mid-hunt.

Clutching his head closer, with my breath coming in shallow gasps I inspected his scalp for the condition plaguing him. There was nothing. No scab, no blood, no puss. Nothing.

In alarm, I glanced around only to find Father's eyes settled on me, his eyebrows so high they were in the edge of his hairline. "Mae, go home at once," he snapped.

I turned around and begun to clear my mess with shaking hands, but his bellow made me jump. "Now!" he boomed.

Without a backward glance at the now healed Aeneid, I scurried for our round house on the edge of the settlement. Bigger than most, it had a flock of trainee priests in the garden tending my herbs. I ran past them, my robe streaming behind. In the house, I slammed the uneven door and stood panting, my back pressed against the wood. What had happened out there? A wild glance at my hand revealed my scabby palm. Some of the crusty welts were already becoming smaller and disappearing but others were still clear to see.

I'd transferred Aeneid's festering infection from his head to my hands, all with the utterance of two words I didn't know. I couldn't even remember them if I tried.

Magic.

Heather's words by the river came back to me—not that

they'd ever been far away—and I stared in wonder at my hands.

Could the old magic run in me? Why?

The door pushed from behind and I jumped out of the way as Father strode in. Pushing back the hood on his cloak he frowned at me. "Mae? What was that I saw?"

I expected him to be cross, but he seemed oddly delighted. A spark flickered to life in the depths of his gaze.

"I don't know, Father, I promise I didn't do anything intentionally." I kept my hands behind my back, but I knew it was futile. Silently he nodded for me to show them and reluctantly I lifted them forward. The scabs were smaller yet again, but they were still there. I breathed through my mouth. I couldn't believe I'd done it. It was impossible.

"It is as I hoped, our answer from the gods is coming." Father clutched my hands, turning them in the dim light to see the yellow crusts of skin better.

"What have you been asking of the gods?"

His eyes flashed. "Come with me." Gesturing for me to follow, he stole out of the door and I ran to keep up with his determined steps. I wrapped my hands in the folds of my dress, hiding the remaining disfiguring sores and followed his trail into the forest.

When we neared the stones, I sighed in dismay. "Not these again, Father. I've told you I don't agree."

His hands swept towards the sky. Stood amongst his circular monument, he fulfilled the true imagery of our priests of old. A crackle of thunder boomed above our heads. My eyes skittered to the stones, taking in my view as I stared at scattered bones, some still meshed with decaying flesh. "What have you done?" I asked him.

He followed my fixed look to the bones. "A few sacrifices to appease the gods."

My legs wobbled, my palms slicking with moisture. I rubbed them on my dress, forgetting the disgusting scabs. "Appease them for what?"

He laughed, "Can't you see, Mae? We are starving down to the last child. Our settlement grows with newcomers, those lost or displaced by the invaders, yet we can't feed them. It's got to end."

"And sacrificing the few animals we have, helps how?"

His mouth crimped into a furious line, brows knotting together, and he stepped toward me. "Tell me what you know."

I backed away a step. "I don't know anything, you know that. I'm the worst student in history."

"You lie."

"Excuse me." I straightened myself to my full height. When I made the effort, I was nearly as tall as him, my willowy frame giving me an unusual height for a woman. "I don't lie. I don't understand what I know."

Sighing, he sat on one of the stones and patted the hard surface. I lowered myself next to him reluctantly. The stone seemed to warm at my touch. I ran my hands along their surface. I couldn't admire them knowing animals had lost their life on them, yet a deep calmness settled in my chest when I touched them. The necklace under my dress heated as it did when I saw Tristram.

Closing my eyes, I allowed the security of the stones to hold me in their grasp. Instead of the darkness I expected behind my closed lids, I was met with a brightness as if I were under the sun on a mountain top. I breathed the fresh air rushing my lungs.

"Your knowledge. I sense from you a great under-standing."

His words pulled me from the mountain top and the

fresh scents of evergreen, healthy with vitality; and into the golden forest in which we were sat, where summer was fading and the harsh realities of winter crept its bitter touch towards us.

"I didn't do anything, Father." I stared up at him, unwilling for him to think I was up to no good. Yes, I may be a poor student, but I never tried to be a bad daughter. "I didn't try to make it happen."

From under robust brows he watched me intently, before leaning in and nudging his shoulder against mine—the most fatherly action he'd made towards me in a while. "These things, we never ask for them."

I didn't speak. I watched and waited. His face smoothed into that far away expression he held when he mentally dipped into the wealth of knowledge only he owned. Unlike when I was a child, when I'd cross my legs and await eagerly for his words, I remained ramrod straight.

"In the times past, magic and reality entwined themselves, one thread of gold, weaving itself with the red of the other. Tightly bound they wound themselves into the fabric of the existence of our forebears." I leant a little closer. "Close your eyes, Mae." I did, my eyelashes fluttering shut. "The gold thread contained the energy, the power of magic. From the earth, it sourced the good fortune of ancient races of men, guiding them to fertile lands, bringing harvests, bountiful fruits, the right water to drink when others would have made us sick.

"While the red was man himself, running with blood and flesh, it bent to the will of man. Following the deepest darkest desires of the human soul."

With my eyes closed, the golden energy warmed in my veins. "What happened?"

Unwillingly, I opened my eyes, losing my vision of the

virile twisting gold and red threads within the depth of my imagination.

"Red and gold can't exist for long in peace." His bright eyes settled on my face, his hand reaching for mine and squeezing my fingers. My stomach clenched, a deep unease settling in the pit of my tummy.

"Why?"

He turned his attention to the trees. Scorched and burned they stared back remorse, their glorious palace of strength brought down by my father's arrangement of the stones. "Because man wants to control everything and any power they don't understand will be extinguished."

"But the threads were closely entwined?" In my vision they seemed to be equal, supporting one another almost.

His fingers squeezed mine. "Until men realised the power those containing the magic held. Then they wanted it themselves, unwilling to leave things as they were, they sought it, wanted to control it."

"Do you feel the magic?" I bit on my bottom lip with my question.

Slowly he shook his head. "No, the skill was lost a long time ago. I can guide it, as can that Kneel Woman, but I don't have it within me. I'm the High Priest because I sense it. I'm closer to it than most, so Alen keeps me close to hand; better to have the power men crave as close as possible."

I didn't correct him and remind him Alen was dead. Tristram would now be the one keeping him close.

Surprising me, he laughed, tilting his head back and shouting into the trees. "But now we have it returned."

"Me?" I backed away a little, but he held my fingers tight.

"You, my child. It is more than I ever dreamed." His eyes sparked with excitement. "Do you know what this means?

You can help us prevent famine, you can lead us to fight these invaders. You hold the future of our people in your hands."

I shied away. "No, Father, Tristram does."

His eyebrows knotted, his hands clenching. "You cannot tell Tristram of this."

"Why?" Forcing myself free, I jumped from the stone. My connection with it didn't end. Just as it had warmed me as I sat on its surface, when I pulled away I felt its immovable strength linger deep within my veins.

"Because he is of the red thread. It runs deep within him. It's the red tie to humanity which puts him in charge. Alen was the same. Men who are meant to fight, to lead; their greed knows no bounds. He will find a way to use the magic, to turn it to his needs."

"Why would he have to turn it?" I whirled, my hands clenching into fists. "I would willingly guide him, help him. Give it to him."

"No." Father's barked word doused the fire in my heart. "Those of the red can't be helped. Can't be guided. They are and always will be guided by their greed and misunderstanding of the complicated balance between right and wrong."

"But, Tristram wasn't meant to lead us, he was the second son."

Father scorned me with a brutal laugh. "You've a lot to learn, Mae. The will of man, the thread of red and blood always fulfils its own purpose. If Tristram is now our leader, then it was always meant to be so."

"Bu—"

He held his hand. "Forget your childish fancies, Mae. Your path is now no longer yours. You shall grow great, you shall guide us."

I went to argue but the deep grooves etched into his forehead told me there was little point. "I won't use my skills to hurt him. He will always be my friend."

Father shook his head. "He will always now be your enemy. He will kill you when he realises you have more power than him."

"You're wrong." I screamed the words. They tore through my throat. "You are wrong."

He smiled, tight and thin lips, almost a sneer. "I am never wrong. You, daughter may have the power of magic within you, but I can sense where it goes, and I can call it where I want."

"You didn't even know I had it."

He laughed. "Didn't I?"

I stumbled at his question. "You said magic was gone, the gold thread had been extinguished by the red."

"And now it's back in you, Mae." He rose his hands to the sky. "It's returned in my daughter; our race of Druids will survive through you, and man will fall at our feet."

Unable to stay and listen, I gathered my skirts into my hands and ran deep into the forest, my heart screaming in my chest. I only stopped when I splashed into the clear crystal waters. Soaking my dress, the chilled depths tugged around my ankles and I threw myself towards them. Red strands of my hair spread around me in a halo as I sank under the surface. Watching them fan in a vibrant array I wondered how part of me could be so red, when within me, even in the depths of deep blue water I could feel so golden.

14

When I woke I was tangled in his arms. It was awkward, but it should have felt a lot more so. My skirt was on the floor, and I'd slept in a t-shirt of his—which smelled somewhere close to heaven—and my panties. His hand rested on my thigh, and his breath inhaled and exhaled gently from his mouth into my ear. Being in his room thirteen hadn't stopped the dreams.

Light stole through his curtains and I knew I needed to somehow de-tangle myself from his embrace and get back to the girls' dorm before we were discovered. While we had done nothing other than talk—the most intimate moment being when he kissed me on the cheek and wished me a good sleep—my night spent in Tristan Prince's arms was unlike any I'd had in the previous eighteen years.

"How did you sleep?" His arms tightened for a moment around my body before releasing and stretching. He smelled of delicious crumpled cotton sheets and still the hint of pine and forest.

"Uh, better I think. I still dreamed though."

With warm fingers he lifted my chin so he could see my

face. Golden stubble lined his jaw, and his hair was a nest of havoc—but then I hadn't seen my own yet.

"Me too."

"Things are changing for them. What did you see?"

It was insane talking about it. But at the same time oddly reassuring.

"Mae is keeping her distance, and he..." Tristan hesitated, "He is hurt. It's a lot to take in being in charge, and he misses her. Misses their moments together."

His dark gaze settled on my face. "What did you see?"

"Mae has magic." I said it.

"Do you?" His gaze was serious despite the ridiculous path our conversation was traveling down.

"No!" I laughed, but I remembered the golden flow of energy and how familiar it had felt. My smile dropped. "Is it us? Have we met before? I still can't believe it."

He shifted, rolling me under him until I was caged in his arms. My heart squeezed and my mouth dried. "I—" He didn't get to say anything else because the door flew open and Mrs Cox loomed in the doorway, the look on her face one of shock and dismay.

He dropped his head onto the pillow next to mine. "Shit."

♊

We walked in silence through the echoing hallways. Five times I went to speak, glancing in his golden direction. Five times I stopped—not knowing what to say.

'Hey, look at us! We dream about one another in a different time. Oh, and also I slept in your room, and it was magical even though we barely touched'.

Silence was better. I'd survived the day without seeing

him after Mrs Cox had dragged me back to the girls wing and left him buttoning a shirt over his toned abs. I wouldn't have minded, but it's not like she found us naked. It's not like anything even happened.

At the end of the day, after dinner, I was in my room combing my hair for the awful social. I was going to have to sit through everyone talking about how I'd been found in Tristan Prince's room. There was a knock on the door.

It was him, displaying a wide smile while he relaxed against my doorjamb. "My Lady."

I flushed. "Don't call me that."

He laughed and tugged at my hand. "Don't care. Are we going to this social?"

"Together?"

He shrugged, but his eyes were alive with dancing depths of molten warmth.

He led us back to the main hall and to a doorway off to the side. "The social is in there."

My stomach did all sorts of crazy dancing with his rubbing low words. "This is going to be hideous."

"I think we might have faced worse."

I shook my head and pushed my hand against his chest. "Don't, Tristan. We still don't know anything. This could all still be a weird coincidence." I said it, my words full of convinced rationality—I didn't believe it. Throwing off my worry, I lightened my expression into one of a friendly smile —the kind of things girls would normally do when they met someone they hated and wanted to kill but then decided that they actually might like after all. "So, the social?"

His lips teased at the edges. "It's not a date." His fingers lifted, and I held my breath, but they dropped again sliding into his pocket. "We need to get on the register, otherwise I'll be in more trouble." He grimaced. "And believe me I'm in enough."

I shifted from foot to foot. "I'm sorry. I should have just gone back to my own room. I did tell Mrs Cox it was innocent, and I was only there because I was scared."

"She hates me, don't worry." Tristan seemed almost upbeat about this, so I didn't bother to comment. "Mrs Melerion would happily accept it as a last strike and send me home."

"That doesn't sound like a bad thing."

"I used to think it wouldn't be." His liquid dark gaze drifted over my face and my cheeks warmed. "I'm changing my mind though." The gentle pink in my cheeks flared into a burning inferno.

With a faint smile, he quickly darted his hand from his pocket, trailing his fingertips across the pink sting on my cheekbone. "Also, we can speak to Phil. If anyone can help us she can."

"How's that?"

He winked which made my stomach flip like crazy. "If anyone can crack where to find information on a computer, it's Phil."

I never wanted him to open the door. I could have stood in the hallway suspended in time for all eternity, but he did, and I followed him into what appeared to be a circle of hell.

Phil and Charlie waved when they saw us, and we slipped around the back of the room while Mrs Cox started writing in white chalk along the board. Phil's eyes were wide as saucers as she watched Tristan and I weave through the tables together. When we reached them, I slipped into the spare chair and Tristan turned to grab a rigid grey plastic one from the empty table alongside. Phil nodded at me like a Chinese cat, her glasses slipping. "What does this mean?" She whispered. "First you are caught in bed together, now you are on a date at social?"

I glared and shook my head. "Shush."

Within a broad wink she leaned towards me. "Got it, secret squirrel, you can tell me later."

"What are we doing?" I said louder, and Tristan settled next to me. My leg vibrated with energy as his knee brushed mine and he glanced up, curving a small smile. Phil watched between us with hawk eyes.

"You've missed the film, with whatever you've not been doing." She wiggled her eyebrows which was incredibly uncool, and I made a mental note to give her hell for it later. Charlie sniggered and flicked a glance in the direction of Tristan. "Now we have to answer the pop quiz."

Mrs Cox spun with alarming speed. "That's right Miss Adams and Mr Prince. You have arrived just in time for the best bit." She clapped her hands. "And even better for you, Mae. You haven't seen the film, so you shall answer the test blind."

This was the Scottish idea for a social? For a nation doused in rain you'd think they'd find better indoor pursuits. Tristan knocked my knee. "Lucky for us I've seen the film a few gazillion times." His dark eyes shone in my direction as he leant closer to whisper low in my ear.

"Have you ever been watching though, Mr Prince?" Mrs Cox's shrill voice made us both cringe. How did that woman hear everything?

Looking at her watch she stepped for the desk and picked up a stop watch. "And go." She clacked her heels towards the window, humming a low tune to herself.

I pulled the piece of A4 white paper towards us and began to read.

"Phil, we need your research skills." Tristan's change of subject made me blink. Was he just going to come out and say it here? Like right here, surrounded by a room full of other kids? I glanced around. Most of the students seemed to be partially asleep and no one turned to look at us.

Phil and Charlie both leaned forward. "Share now," Phil demanded.

Tristan didn't seem at all perturbed by Phil's quirkiness. "We need access to records from this area."

Phil's face scrunched with dismay. "Mae, is this about those stones again? I told you they don't exist, my pare—"

"They exist." Tristan shut her off.

"They do?" She pushed her glasses back, as if she were readjusting her bullshit detector.

"I've seen them, and so has Mae."

"Okay, I'll have to talk to Mum and Dad, see what they know. Maybe they didn't tell me everything."

"No, don't tell your parents, Phil, not yet. We need to work out who the skeletons were and what they have to do with Mae and I." His dark gaze paused on my face thoughtfully. "It's too much coincidence we are both here together."

Phil cocked her head to one side. "Normally most things seem sane in comparison to the stuff I spout. But you and these damn stones." She wiggled her finger at me.

"It's not just the stones," I mumbled, and she shifted forward.

"What do you mean?"

Charlie coughed, and we all dropped our heads pretending to look at the quiz as Mrs Cox clacked past in her heels. "You will be here all night the way you girls are talking; isn't that right, Mr Prince?"

Tristan stiffened but lifted his head and flashed her a blinding smile. I watched spellbound. I'd never seen him smile. We'd gone from frowning and strangling to kissing in record time—it hadn't left many opportunities for gazing at his beautiful face.

But, hadn't I seen it before?

Wasn't it in every moment of the tangled dreams chasing me through night and day?

Once Mrs Cox had moved on, he reached and squeezed my hand in full view of Phil and Charlie. Both of their eyes stalked, and Charlie's mouth popped open and closed like a fish out of water.

His touch shot a warm tingle from the palm of my hand to my chest.

Phil grinned. "Come on, tell me what you mean."

My cheeks flared with a gentle burn. "Since I've been here, I've been having these dreams."

Clapping a hand over her mouth, Phil guffawed an echoing snort of laughter. Mrs Cox spun on her heel and glared in our direction.

I shushed her with a wave of my hand. "Not like that, Phil." Tristan's lips smirked momentarily and then settled back into a straight line of concern. "I've been having dreams of another place, people who lived here before."

Phil stared blankly "Maybe it's just an overactive imagination?"

"But they carry on from one another; every night I see the following time span. Dreams aren't organised, are they?"

Charlie dipped her blonde head closer. "What aren't you saying?"

I gulped in some air. This was the crazy bit. If I could just blurt it out, everything would finally be off my chest. "It's me in the dreams." I lifted my face to Tristan's. "And Tristan, it's us in a different life."

Scratching her head, Phil pursed her lips. "Mae, the past is just the past."

Charlie shook her head until it could have rolled off. "No, my grandma always believed in reincarnation. She was always trying to get in touch with her former self."

"And did she?" I leant forward, maybe her grandma could help me.

"Not that I know of. She died when I was eleven."

Falling back in my chair, I sighed before remembering my manners. "Sorry about your grandma."

Charlie shrugged. "She was batshit crazy. Always going on about lives being linked."

Phil scribbled on the sheet as Mrs Cox swept passed again. "I think it's just dreams in that creepy as hell room, Mae."

Tristan coughed. "No, I'm having the dreams too." The table stared at him until Phil rocked back on her chair.

"Tristan 'I'm so Cool' Prince is having dreams about the past?"

His cheeks flared a little with colour under the golden depths of his skin and his mouth crimped into a line. I glared at Phil. "Are you up for helping?" I asked.

She shook her head again, giggling a low snigger. "Okay, okay, I'll help." She glanced at us all. "Let's get this stupid quiz done and then everyone meet back at Mae's."

I shuddered at the thought of being back in that space and Tristan's knee knocked mine. He nodded softly, and I breathed a low breath. "Okay, my room."

"I'll get my laptop and we'll see what we can find."

Charlie slapped the table. "It's town day on Saturday. We can look around that bookshop in the village."

Phil nodded, hooked on the idea of research. "Yeah, that

old lady has books in there no one has bothered to look at for hundreds of years."

This was good. We were getting somewhere. "Everything I've dreamed of so far is linked to the girl in the dreams' magic."

Phil and Charlie's eyes widened—honestly the way this conversation was going they were going to end up with headaches. Phil nodded thoughtfully. "Now we are getting somewhere. Magic history is such a niche. Of course real historians, like my parents, think it's all coddlefoffle."

"All what?" I sniggered.

"A coddlefoffle, you know, nonsense."

Charlie laughed under her breath her shoulders shaking. "Phil, that's not a word."

Phil tilted her head to the side, "Who the hell taught me that then?"

I was in my room waiting for the others. All the lights were on and I was pacing the small cramped space. There was no chance I was going to risk sitting down in case I fell asleep again. Deep in my heart was an ache to know what happened next, to see the version of Tristan again from my dreams. But I had to stay here in the present. I needed to look at the past, to discover it from a distant perspective.

And. And... Far worse than time slipping away before I could discover the true identity of the people from my night-time experience, was the simple fact my heart already knew what happened to them. I knew that somehow they ended up on those stones together.

Time was ticking for them. I could sense it.

Was she really me?

My brain, the part of me who knew I was a girl from Queens with no possessions to my name said no. But my heart, pounding in my chest, said without any doubt, yes.

How, I didn't know.

Why Tristan and I hated each other on sight—I didn't know.

Why the necklace stopped us—I didn't know.

There was a lot I didn't know.

A gentle tap on my window made me jump out of my skin. It only took one step to cross the cramped space. I tugged on the handle expecting it to be stiff, but it unlocked with ease.

Tristan's dark gaze met mine. "Move back so I can jump up."

"Sorry, what?" I stepped back just as he curled his tall frame and launched himself onto the window frame.

"Hey." He straightened, and we stood with a few inches between us. Hands by our sides, we faced one another. The air rippled and shifted. We were nothing more than two strangers placed together within the same school. Two people from different places. Yet, as I watched him— absorbing the smooth skin on his face, the hint of gold stubble along his cheeks, those dark eyes burning with a dense depth—I knew him more than I'd ever known anyone.

With a grin, I held out my hand. "Hi, I'm Mae Adams."

Eyes crinkling with a smile, he met my hand with own. "Tristan Prince."

Stepping back, I sat and patted the edge of the mattress. "A prince?" My tongue felt fat and useless as he settled at my side, our elbows brushing. It was silly when I'd woken tied within his arms.

He smiled, his face shifting to look at me fully. I basked under the intensity of his gaze. "At your service."

"How did you end up here at this awful school?" I wanted to know everything about the guy I felt I already knew.

He shrugged, his wide powerful shoulders rising and falling. "I was told I was going to boarding school. I chose this one."

"You chose this one?"

The expression on his face and his eyes as they danced over my lips made my stomach dip to the bottom of my feet. "I couldn't explain it until now."

"What's that?" My words tangled in my throat.

"It's like we've both been guided here."

I gave a small snort. "I haven't been guided here; my aunt asked me to come." I bristled a little at the thought of my missing aunt. "And then decided I wasn't worth being here to meet."

His fingers grabbed mine, giving them a firm squeeze before linking through and entwining his golden skin with my pale.

Silence enveloped us as we both contemplated our own thoughts. I was the one to break it. "Do you think we are them, or it's just dreams?" I hesitated, unsure if he'd think I was being foolish. But why else were we sat on the edge of my bed holding hands? I didn't know Tristan Prince. We hadn't flirted with one another for weeks before finally summoning the courage to ask the other out on a date. We hadn't texted or had long phone calls about nothing in the middle of the night. We hadn't stared at one another across a classroom while all our friends nudged one another and laughed. That was the normal route. I'd seen it.

But here we were. Just together. I knew I wouldn't change it.

He turned towards me, running a finger along the edge

of my jaw. My skin tingled at its lazy path. "I don't know. But I know you. I can't explain it, Mae, there's no rationality, it's just a simple fact."

I nodded, my mouth too dry to speak. His lips lowered to mine, and I watched them come closer, soft blooms of delicate flesh. My heart pounded, blood rushing in my ears. I caught my breath waiting for his kiss.

"Excuse me." Phil barged through the door and I scowled at her arrival. She plopped her stuff on the bed. Tristan's eyes glanced at mine with a chasing shadow of regret. He moved with a sigh to make room for the whirlwind that was Philomena Potts. "Right, let's get researching. Charlie is waiting in the line for the phone. She's going to ring her mum and see what she remembers of Grandma Crazy's reincarnation ramblings." She unpacked her laptop with the same excitement the average five-year-old would attack a pile of Christmas presents. I chuckled, and she glared. "What can I say, I'm my parents' daughter. Anyway, you can't comment, Miss 'I Want to Talk to the Trees'."

It was my turn to glare. Tristan's heavy stare fell onto me. "Did you feel an affinity with nature before you came here, Mae?" He leaned closer, his words low, his breath fanning over my face.

I flushed. "Well, I wouldn't describe it as an affinity." I glared again at Phil who just shrugged.

"Isn't that like the dreams, though?" Tristan asked.

"I don't know, they are hazy."

His dark gaze widened. "But wouldn't they be hazy if you are remembering a life from thousands of years ago?"

Scrunching my face, I contemplated this. If I was the girl from the dreams, yeah sure it was a long time ago.

"So, you think the dreams are about Druids?" Phil's question made Tristan and I spring apart.

I nodded, thinking hard, trying to push through the dense mist that separated me from the dreams. "I think so. She's wearing red robes, her father white."

"Okay," Phil concentrated on her laptop. "I just need the connection." She pointed at a USB hook-up on the side of her laptop.

"How have you got a laptop with internet, when the rest of us can't even have our cells?"

Winking, she sniggered. "I don't know what laptop you're talking about."

I grinned at her. "Me neither."

Phil laughed. "I think we know that already." She turned back to her laptop and Tristan squeezed my hand.

"You aren't crazy, either that or we both are." Tilting his head to the side he thought for a moment. "I really hope we aren't crazy."

I squeezed his hand. I didn't want to be crazy, but then I also didn't want to know we'd died on those stones, two bodies hugging one another in death.

"Druid magic." Phil spoke out as she typed once the connection was made. I gulped loudly. This was happening. We were exploring the crazy.

The room shrunk, my head whirling.

"The Romans stamped out Druidism in the United Kingdom," Phil said, speaking from within the glare of the laptop screen. "The Druids built the stones as a portal to the gods, to create a connection between the earth and the gods."

My heart thrummed in my chest. "Yes, I think they are coming for us." Closing my eyes, I felt around me trying to reach into the dreams. I sighed, centring myself. A gentle hum of gold spread from my heart through my veins until it felt as though my blood were gold not red. "There's an army. They want to bring back magic and create a force while they rule over all the isles."

An army of red marched in the depths of my memory. Golden spears held aloft, they carved a path through the lands, always looking for one thing. At the head, leading the march was a cavernous darkness. Endlessly deep and evil, it ruthlessly turned those aside who it wasn't seeking.

My eyes flew open. Tristan and Phil watched me intently. My hand squeezed Tristan's so tight his skin bleached white. "The Roman's weren't expanding their empire, they were searching for magic."

Phil's mouth dropped. "You can't know that."

My gaze met hers, my heart thrumming. I knew what I knew, even though I couldn't explain it. "I do. They weren't coming for slaves and land. They were coming for her."

I stood, my eyes gazing out the window. The forest called for me. *Come find yourself.* The stones, they wanted me.

When I turned back to the room, my body flowed with an indescribable strength. "They were coming for me. The stones, they harnessed the magic." I'd felt it when I'd touched them. I remembered how it had felt when I'd seen the images from my dreams in the flesh. The scent of the earth, the birds in the air. The world was young, the stones were young, untouched by wear and tear.

Turning, I ran from the room, rushing down corridors until I found the fresh damp air outside. The stones they needed me, and I wasn't going to say no.

My clothes were torn, my bare feet bleeding when I found them in the dark inky night air. I fell to the ground and placed my hands on the stone containing the bones. A deep crack split the air, a yawning high-keening cry.

I smiled. The stones had what they wanted. Me.

15

S trange that the place I hid from my father was within his circle of stones. He'd look for me in the forest or by the water, and I needed the air to breathe that being around him made impossible.

Since he'd discovered the golden magic I contained, he'd been nothing but the attentive father I'd missed over the last years.

I wanted to please him. But his new rules were hard to obey.

No time with Tristram.

No open magic in front of the other villagers.

Instead, endless hours of practice behind the closed door of our house.

My back rubbed against the smooth stone, cool and comforting. It was as though it provided an anchor to a nameless quantity I needed.

"Mae!" I groaned as my name was called yet again. Placing my hands on the earth scattered with crisp and curling leaves, I felt for who it was. It was a trick I still couldn't fully understand, but the earth could tell me the identity of someone approaching quicker than my ears.

Deacon.

I stood and brushed at my woollen dress. With winter fast approaching, all the villagers with the means were using their warmer clothes. It counterbalanced for the chill our lack of food left on our bodies.

Deacon grinned as he stepped through the clearing of trees and held his hands above his head, palms towards me. "I come in peace."

I didn't know what he spoke of, but Deacon always made me smile. "Have you done something wrong to need to declare peace?"

He stepped closer and I cast an enquiring look over his face. He seemed tired. While his lips were quirked in his easy smile, the skin around his eyes was pinched and thin. "You seem to have fallen into a foul mood with Tristram. I wasn't sure if you extended your new animosity to his friends as well."

My stomach plummeted at the mention of Tristram's name. It was the one rule of my father's I couldn't withstand. Tristram had given up casting hurt glances my way five days before, and now he only looked at me with scorn and disregard when I stood with Father as my parent gave him priestly advice. It hurt.

"You are my friend too, are you not?" I tried hard to wipe the despondency off my face. No one knew what I was going through apart from Father.

"Of course." Deacon nodded, and I smiled.

"How can I help?"

He shifted a little from one side to another. "I remembered what you did with Agnese's baby when she had such difficulty birthing the bairn."

I flushed. "I did little. It is Heather who knows such things." I peered at him closer. "What's wrong, Deacon?"

His skin paled to a chalky white and he coughed uneasily. "Arethia has not had her woman's curse for three cycles of the moon." His cheeks flamed with dots of vivid pink and he shifted from foot to foot. "But today she starts to bleed. She wants you, she thinks you can help."

I cringed. "Deacon, the bairn won't stay in place if it doesn't want to." It was a wretched thing to have to say. The whole settlement knew their private anguish at being married so long with no child to show of it.

"Please, Mae."

I shook my head. "Call on Heather, she knows more."

"No one has seen Heather for weeks, she comes and goes as she likes."

I frowned. I also hadn't seen the Kneel Woman, not since we spoke by the river. "Deacon—"

"And if your chief demanded it?" I was pleased to see his face cringe with shame as he pulled his final trick.

I sighed. "If my chief demands then I shall come. Tristram could have come to get me himself if he so wished; if he wasn't running around with a wounded pride like a spoilt child. Come, let's go."

We turned back for the settlement and I held my head high as we walked through the villagers to Deacon's hut. I knew people were whispering about me since Father had all but hidden me from view. I figured they all thought I was being punished for not completing my studies. What they didn't know was I had completed my studies—overnight. I knew everything now my Father knew, and more.

I pushed through the doorway, stepping into the dim smoky light of Deacon's home. "Arethia," I called softly, stepping further into the room.

"She's in there." Deacon pointed behind a curtain but backed away, his hand still holding onto the door at the entrance.

"Go." I nodded to the freedom of outside, he'd be happier out there.

He turned and slipped out the door, pulling it closed behind him and leaving me in a deep gloom. Arethia groaned behind the curtain and swallowing a deep swallow of air I stepped through. Fetid air caught the back of my throat and I blinked a few times to accustom my sight. Arethia writhed on the bed coverings. They were dark and damp with her sweat, and her hair stuck to her forehead, her face creased in pain.

"Oh, Arethia, come." I bent over the poor girl, her clammy skin pressing into the palm of my hand. I smoothed over her forehead. "The pain will pass, I promise."

Her wild eyes found mine. "Don't let me lose it, My Baduri. Please, My Lady, Deacon will be so torn."

"It's just nature, Arethia. You can't stop nature, no matter how much we may wish."

"Call on the gods, give them anything to make them help me."

I smiled gently. "I don't think it works like that."

She groaned again, lifting her hips off the mattress. I kept one hand on her forehead while I placed the other on her tummy. It was soft to my touch, the hardened swell of pregnancy not yet arrived.

There was nothing for me to do other than comfort her in her moment of desperate need. Closing my eyes, I willed a calm to ease her sore body and fractured mind. For a girl so young, she'd been through too much.

Settling myself to stay till the end, I emptied my thoughts, allowing the swirl of gold to expand in my mind. It was always there, the gold my father had described as a thread of magic weaving in my veins, but it was only when I called it to the surface of my thoughts I could feel its full intensity.

I imagined it weaving through my body, pounding and mixing with my blood until I was only gold.

My hand warmed against Arethia's belly, much like it had over Agnese's all those weeks ago when I hadn't known what I contained within me. That day had been the start of everything.

It would be so lovely for Arethia to hold a bube in her slender arms, she wished it so much. An overwhelming sense of sadness filled my chest and a tear slipped down my cheek, swiftly followed by another.

My hand heated and the gem at my throat vibrated. Under my touch Arethia's belly hardened. This was it, the final contraction before the small unformed babe would be passed. I waited for Arethia's cry and the contraction of her slender frame, but it never came.

Opening my eyes, I blinked at the room. A pale light filled the dim space, as if the sun were streaming through an open window. "Arethia? How do you feel? I'll help you clean up."

Raising onto elbows, she stared directly in my face. "My baby is still there."

"It can't be, Arethia. It's passing. I'm sorry you've gone through this again, but there will be more times, I can assure you."

She shook her head. "No, it's there, I can feel it."

I frowned. I didn't know much about pregnancy, but I knew the quickening didn't happen for a long while. "It's just the cramps," I explained.

She shook her head, her face splitting into a smile, tears leaking from the corners of her eyes. "No. Feel." She grabbed my hand and placed it onto the gentle curve of her tummy. Sure enough, a roll from under its surface pressed into my palm. "It's a miracle from the gods. Whatever you promised them, I will pay. I swear on my life, we will pay whatever the price was to have this child."

I shook my head, trying to reassure her. "Arethia, I didn't ask the gods; it seemed too late."

Her eyes widened. "Then it was you."

I shook my head and smiled, patting her belly with gentle fingers. "Maybe it's the baby itself? Maybe he will grow to be our greatest warrior yet."

She smiled through her delirious tears. "Maybe." But I knew she didn't agree with me. She thought it was me, and truthfully, I no longer knew what was me and what wasn't.

Had I stopped Arethia from losing her baby, or had I just been there at the right time?

"Can you keep this between us?" I asked.

A flicker of confusion creased her brow, but she nodded. "Anything, My Baduri."

I smiled and stood from my spot on the edge of the mattress. "I'm just Mae."

She nodded her agreement and settled back on the bed, her face glowing. But I could see in the depth of her eyes she no longer thought I was 'just Mae'.

So, who the hell was I?

I avoided the curious glances of the villagers who were all stood waiting for the bad news of Arethia's fate and slipped around the edge of their hut. Within me it was as though a torrid storm whirled a path of destruction. I wanted to run. I wanted to stay. Seemed I didn't know what I wanted.

A crack of a twig pulled me from my tortured thoughts. Tristram was stood a little way off. His facial expression mirrored the way I twisted and turned on the inside. I wanted him to come forth to speak with me, but he knew I'd cut myself off from him. He wasn't brave enough to come ask why, and I resented the fact he wouldn't fight to speak.

He nodded once, stiff and proud, and I returned the motion. Then I walked away with my head held high and my heart crashing in my chest.

"Hey, Sister?"

I turned at the sound of Alana and made room for her on the log bridge. One of our favourite spots as children, we'd had wild afternoons in the sunshine daring one another to walk across the fast current of the river along the fallen log. Now I was sat here, and the echoed giggles of those children were lost to the time of another life. "Hello." I smiled up at her.

"Deacon is declaring you a miracle worker." She blinked at me through her long golden eyelashes. Pale and creamy, her skin bore no mark from the passing summer days, not like my own which was blemished with splatters of freckles.

"I'm not a miracle worker." I assured her. "It could have been anything causing the bleed, maybe she was never going to lose the baby at all." I shrugged. "How am I supposed to know what will be?"

Alana watched me carefully and her fingers gripped mine. "But you do know, don't you, Mae?" She sighed, and a flicker of frustration crossed her face. "Couldn't you just close your eyes and discover what the future holds for us?"

I rolled my eyes. "I'm not a seeing lake, Alana, merely a person."

"*Father thinks you are far more than any person.*"

I grunted. "*Father has much more time for me these days, too much if you ask me.*"

"*But isn't he helping?*"

I considered this for a brief pause. "*Maybe. It's hard to tell. He wants to know everything I know.*"

"*What do you know?*"

Obviously, Alana, bright flame as she was, wasn't unaware of the changes within me, nor the change in my parental relationship.

I shrugged, my shoulders lifted high, but then they stayed there with tension. "*I don't know. I know stuff: like I know the isles once didn't belong together; that this island we call our own, once belonged to land nearer where our enemies come from.*"

"*And who are our enemies?*" Her serious pale blue eyes reflected the turmoil etched on my own face. "*The Druia? Are they going to attack? We are receiving more and more displaced people every day. It seems nowhere is safe.*"

I closed my eyes, dipping deep within the vast well of golden energy humming in my chest. "*No, the Druia want peace, they are worried.*"

My hand automatically splayed onto the log, my fingernails digging into the surface. The log was dead and had been for a long, long while, but the moss and creeping weeds which scattered over its surface thrummed with vitality. I reached towards them seeking answers. The water of the river slowed beneath our swinging feet.

"*They march through the southern lands.*" I could see them in my mind, hear the vicious stamp of feet, the pull and whirl of wheeled chariots carrying supplies. "*They carve the land, creating their own straight roads, ignoring our ancient ways.*"

Alana squeezed my hand and I cast my thoughts further afield. Ebrehered of the Druia clan was sat by a fire; wrapped in animal skins he stared into the flames. His head bent towards a slender shape in a black cloak, a woman it must have been with that fragile frame. Her head tilted so I couldn't see her face, but beneath the edge of her hood was grey hair.

"Ebrehered talks with a stranger. She wants to know who we are and what we have here."

"What's he telling her?" Alana prompted without need. I was already searching what I could see.

"He doesn't want to tell her anything." Just then I saw him motion a large rectangle shape with his hands. The stones—Father's stones—he was telling her of them. I gasped loudly, clutching my hand to my mouth. As if she heard me, the woman turned and stared at my vantage point. It was madness, because I knew she couldn't see me, but I felt her seeking glance all the way down to my bones, and the flitting smile which grazed her lips set a chill across my skin. Her hand flew in my direction and I was severed from the image. Crying out, I toppled off the log and into the rapid river below.

Shocked by the icy pull of the current, I splashed and flailed. Alana shouted from above but from under the water all I could hear was a muffled bleat. The image of the woman's face chased me down to the river bed, my dress dragging my helpless body.

Water gushed in my mouth, rushing up my nose, and my ears built with painful pressure. The woman's face, I knew it from somewhere. It teased me as I screwed my eyes shut against the floating black dots drifting across my eyes. I was going to die in the river I'd played in as a child.

The next thing I knew I was on the bank. My lungs

screamed for air, my chest heaving, as I choked on water rushing out of my mouth.

"Mae," Alana's scream tore through the air, and my head landed in her lap as she rolled me over.

"I'm fine." But, I wasn't fine. I was burning from the inside out. "Thank you for pulling me out." I gasped around my words.

Her eyes were wide orbs. "I didn't, Mae, I didn't." She sobbed, her chest rising and falling, the patter of her tears mixing with the river water on my skin.

I reached for her face, cupping my hand around her cheek. Two motherless sisters tied together with love. "There is magic in my veins."

She sobbed a bit harder. "I know. Don't you think I know?"

A wild sob of my own clamoured up my throat. "I never wanted this."

"Shh." She soothed my hair. "It wanted you."

My chest tightened, the vision all too clearly coming back to me. "I don't think magic is the only thing that wants me."

"No?"

She leaned down closer, her skin smelled of comfortably familiar lavender water. Water that I distilled for her with my own hands. "Someone is coming. And it's me she's searching for."

Alana's eyes hardened. "Who? When?"

I shook my head. "I don't know. I just feel it."

She sat in silence for a moment, her thoughts deep.

"We will keep you safe. I know Tristram will keep you safe."

That strangling sob tightened my throat again. "Father won't let me tell him anything. He says I can't trust him."

Alana clucked her tongue against the roof of her mouth

but didn't speak ill against our parent. "You need to tell him what you saw."

I shook my head. "I don't want to."

"Then what are you going to do?" Her pale-blue gaze searched my face, the ivory skin around her eyes creasing with concern. I pushed myself up. It was futile to wallow in regret. I may not understand who I was, but I had to embrace it.

"I will help our people. I will always help our people, even if it takes my last breath." Standing, I, kicked my wet dress away from my chilled legs. "I'm going to tell Father I want to use my magic for good. He can't allow for me to not use it when we are in such desperate need. Have you seen poor Mary's leg? It oozes with poison. It will kill her soon unless it heals."

Alana's face stayed calm, but a waver shook her voice. "And you can heal Mary of poison?"

"By the god's I will try."

I reached for Alana's hand. Her own clothes were also wet now from my hair. We wrapped our arms tight around one another's waist and walked back towards the settlement. I knew where I would find Father.

There he was. Standing amongst his precious stones. As I stepped closer, a high-pitched wail screamed within my ears. I turned, expecting to see a child running through the trees, injured. The noise was so debilitating I placed my hand onto the nearest stone to steady myself.

Daylight vanished as if I were in a swoon and the night stars winked down at me. Then the deafening crack split the air and the earth shuddered, and all time spun.

16

My hand sunk into the earth and I heaved, my stomach squeezing tight and my skin breaking out in a chilled sweat. I shivered beneath the wet clothes clinging to my legs.

Trying to stand, my legs shook so much I fell onto my ass in the dirt. Shaking fingers felt my face, my hair. The universe shifted as I breathed a sigh of relief. I was me. Mae Adams. But, I was wearing her clothes. The wool weighed heavy with water from her dousing in the river.

I gasped. Every moment was real. The dress was wet. It wasn't a dream. Scurrying across the soil I glared at the stones. They were the same, unmoving, as they had been for thousands of years.

I couldn't bring myself to think it.

Could I?

My gulping swallow lodged in my throat.

I'd walked through the stones.

I'd walked through the stones and become her.

I shook my head. That wasn't right. It wasn't true. I stared at the stars as I contemplated the enormity of the truth. They shone down, urging me on. What were they saying? They'd always been there? The same stars over my head.

I'd walked through the stones and I was her.

I *was* her.

"Miss Adams?"

I screeched at the surprising call of my name, blinking into the looming darkness. I expected it to be Tristan. *Tristram.* They were one and the same. Same as her and I were the same.

We were the same people living a different life.

But I knew this to be right. Souls came around again. It was what I'd been taught to believe... but it wasn't me taught that. It was her.

I locked the thought away as a shadowy form slipped through the shadows. "Don't be scared, Miss." I blinked like a startled animal at Jeffries, the chauffeur, as he came closer. He was dressed in a thick coat and gum boots. "We've been searching for you for days." He dropped to a crouch on the ground. The earth rumbled beneath my hands. Was it a warning? I didn't know. Should I be running?

But Jeffries of the facial hair fame had never threatened me. I'd hardly seen him since I'd arrived. I'd hardly seen anyone. I'd been sleeping and dreaming. My heart boomed in my chest.

Not dreaming. *Remembering.*

"What do you mean days?" I shook my head trying to give myself some space to get my brain engaged and working.

"It's Sunday, Miss. You've been missing for five days."

I stared at the stones I'd gone through. As crazy as it sounded, I knew I'd walked through the ancient stones into Mae's life. Yet it had only been a day. Hadn't it?

The sound of crashing footsteps through the forest made me spin. Tristan, his face pale, the shadows under his eyes bruised and deep, rushed into view. "Thank God." He fell onto his knees in the space before me. His fingers slid around my face, his thumbs brushing across my cheeks.

It was madness. A few days before we'd hated one another. Now, my lungs ached to be beside him, staggering to draw breath because the beating of my heart was so deep. "Tristram," I whispered his real name and the depth of dark longing in his gaze told me he understood. He got it too.

If that was him and I on those stones, tangled together in a deathly embrace we'd died loving one another. The purple gem at my throat heated and pulsed against my skin. Was that why Heather the Kneel Woman had given it to Mae? I shook as I stared wildly into Tristan's face. "I've found out so much," I whispered.

He smoothed my hair and leant close. "Shh, let's get you back and checked over." He pulled me from the ground with a gentle tug. "Can you walk?" He moved as if he planned to pick me up, but I waved him off.

"No, I'm fine."

One of his arms slipped around my waist tight, and Jeffries flanked my other side. I didn't know how many of them they thought they'd need to catch me if I stumbled, but I was too tired to argue. Shuddering waves of exhaustion threatened to pull me down, and I was grateful of Tristan's supportive arm.

The castle loomed into view. Despite its crumbling façade, when I looked hard at it I sensed it was there for a purpose. The foundations which I knew delved deep into the soil had stood on that site for hundreds of years for a reason. The environment had absorbed the castle into its very fabric. The castle was linked to the stones, I just knew.

Was it protecting them from being found, or hiding them from being found by the wrong people?

Hadn't Phil told me her parents had searched and searched but found nothing?

My head whirled.

Had they been waiting for me?

Had the castle been waiting for me to step through its doors?

Why?

And why... I glanced with apprehension at the man by my side. Why was Tristram here with me at the same time?

My eyes flickered with black spots, and my knees quaked.

"Nearly there." Tristan held me tighter, his chest pushing against my rib cage as he took all my weight.

We were through the wide arched doorway when shouts drifted towards us. "Take her to the sick bay," the shrill broad voice of Mrs Cox called. I fluttered in and out of darkness as Tristan weaved through more corridors I hadn't yet ventured down. When I landed on a hard yet soft surface I kept my eyes shut.

How could I face reality? What was reality?

"Mae?" A brush of breath fanned across my skin. "Look at me."

I stared straight into the midnight depths of Tristan's gaze, and within their inky pools it was as though I could lose my soul. "Where have you been?" He squeezed my fingers.

I blinked a few times, trying to formulate a response which wasn't on the far side of insanity. I couldn't think of one. "The past," was all I muttered before the clack of Mrs Cox's heels announced her arrival. Tristan didn't back away as the force that was the tiny Scot breezed into the cavernous sick bay.

"Mae," Mrs Cox's clipped tone was tightened like a violin string. I couldn't look at her, so I feigned unconsciousness. I didn't know what to say to anyone, so maybe it was best if I said nothing at all.

I don't know how long I slept for, drifting in and out of dark dreams. Although what were dreams and what was reality I no longer knew. When I closed my eyes, Tristram was there watching me, his dark gaze questioning and filled with distrust the further she, or me, pulled away from him. No matter how much I pulled away from the dreams, tried to stay within the light of day, they pulled me back until I was no longer sure I'd walked back through the stones at all —maybe that was the dream.

Every so often firm fingers would squeeze mine. Lips brushed my hair and my heart pounded with the thunder of wild horses. He never spoke as I battled to find reality. He was there though and mixed within my dreams, the purple gem at the base of my throat warmed with comforting familiarity.

"You do realise," it was Phil's voice who spoke, but in my head it mixed with the smile of Alana. "You can't miss English forever. Eventually you are going to have to stand up and give your verdict on Romeo and Juliet to Mrs Barlow."

I laughed, chasing Alana down towards the river. We were closer now, closer than we had been while the secret of my power was hidden. "Anything that ends with the death of two young lovers isn't worth reading," I told her, but she frowned in confusion.

"Wake me up, Phil." Tears burned my eyes, and I blinked them away until they were captured on delicate lips. *Tristan.*

"That's enough." A sharp clap shattered the air, and I blinked at the ceiling above. Even in the deepest darkest dreams, Mrs Cox could still make her presence known. "You can't miss your whole birthday."

I blinked towards her voice. I wanted to see my friend, wanted to see Tristan, but only a shadowy shape waited for me by the side of the bed.

"Heather?" I gasped. My head whirled. "Birthday?"

"Oh, my goodness, child, I have never known anyone make things as complicated as you."

Sleep evaporated, my dreams chased off back into the past. It couldn't be my birthday. That was still days away. How long had I been asleep? "Mrs Cox? *Heather?*"

The small round eyes of Mrs Cox rolled. "You remember me then?"

"I've dreamed about you." I managed to haul myself into a semi-upright position, although my head was none too pleased.

"Dreamed? Remembered you mean, Mae."

Her words came back to me from the day of my arrival. *Your ancestors came from here; your blood will remember.* "It wasn't my ancestors who came from here was it?"

Mrs Cox, or who I now plainly saw as Heather, the Kneel Woman from two thousand years ago, shook her head, a small smile playing on her lips. "Well they did, but so did you."

"And you're still alive because you're a superhuman witch?"

She snorted and perched a slender hip on the edge of the sick bay bed. "I'm not a witch, Mae."

"No?"

"No, I'm a conduit for energy. I can sense it, feel it, and sometimes if I'm very lucky, guide it."

"But you have been alive forever."

Another uncharacteristic eye-roll. "No. But I tied myself to here, so I could be here when you got back home."

"But it was my aunt who called me back?" I narrowed my eyes. "Does she know about my dreams, about who I was before?" Then it came to me. "There is no aunt is there?"

The cool fingers of Mrs Cox landed on my hand and patted. "I can be ingenious when required."

"Like when you made Mae help with Agnese's baby, even though she didn't know what she was doing?"

"You, *you* didn't know what you were doing." Her smile was all knowing, and I bristled.

"How did you know where to find me? How did you know I was an orphan in Queens?"

"I felt you from when your soul came back. I always knew it would cycle back when the time was right." She nodded. "Admittedly I didn't expect to wait so long."

"Sorry," I grumbled. "Didn't mean to make you wait around."

Mrs Cox leaned closer. "It was worth the wait, but you're in trouble. Soon they will know you are back and they will come for your magic once again."

"Why am I back now, if you've been waiting all this time?"

Heather/Mrs Cox, peered at me, her face sombre. "You and Tristram were cursed on the stones. You were never meant to find one another again." She shrugged. "This is the first cycle you've both been back at the same time." A knowing smile stretched across her face. "I guessed you wouldn't be able to stay apart."

"So that's why he chose this school?"

"What can I say; he's a Clans man through and through." She laughed a little and from under the image of Mrs Cox I could see the gap-toothed smile of Heather, her bracelets jingling.

"Is that why we hated one another?"

She raised an eyebrow and I flushed when I remembered the way she'd found us the morning before. She touched the gem at my throat. "You just needed a connection to remember one another."

If my head hadn't hurt so much I would have laughed. As it was, my brain resembled a bowling ball rolling around my head, so I kept still and my laughter at a minimum. "I don't have magic, so why would someone come for it?"

"Don't you?"

I groaned. "Why are you always so cryptic? You are cryptic in my dreams—"

"Memories," she cut in, her face pinching beneath her glasses.

"Whatever: dreams, memories, it all feels the same."

She slid from the bed, readjusting her shirt and skirt. She was nothing like the Heather I may have known before. "You should know, you aren't alone."

I stared at her blank face. "Why do you always talk in riddles?"

"Mae, I can guide you. I've waited a long time to make sure I can help." Her lips pursed for a short pause. "But, I can't lead you."

"Why?" My hands fisted the cotton of the bed sheet.

She smiled and beneath the sparrow form of Mrs Cox, Heather grinned back at me. "Because you are our leader."

"In what?"

If someone didn't give me an answer soon, I'd implode with questions.

"The old ways. You hold their future, it was always your gift."

My face scrunched. "The old ways? Not those damn stones?" I shuddered when I thought of Mae and Tristram tied together in their final embrace.

"Older."

"And Tristram? Why did we both die?" The necklace pulsed as my thoughts scattered in his direction. "Is the necklace to help us find one another?"

A small frown carved itself between her eyebrows. "No. I gave you the necklace that day, so you'd find yourself again."

"So you knew I'd die?" It was my turn to frown. "Jeez, some heads-up would have been nice."

"I don't know anything. I'm a conduit, not a seer." Her glance was pointed. "You are the one with the power."

"Power for what?"

"Everything."

I stared at my hands. If there was power—magic— beneath my skin, I didn't know how to access it or what to do with it. Those memories hadn't come back yet, and when I'd walked through the stones, I hadn't seen anything more.

"How can I walk through the stones?"

"You and Tristram sacrificed yourselves so your father wouldn't get your power. Tristram was never meant to be with you on those stones. Your father cursed you both on the chance your souls would ever meet again. But I believe

the tie of your blood shifted the allegiance of the stones—
they have been waiting for you as long as I have."

Her lips quirked into a grin. "But nothing can stay in
the way of gold and red united. Not even a power-hungry
druid keen to control the universe with magic."

"Tristram died for me?" My mouth tingled and dried.
"Is that why? Because her father wanted to steal my power."
I shuddered. "I would have given it to him to save Tristram."

Heather/Mrs Cox shook her head. "*Your* father." She
let her words sink in. "You can't ever allow the magic to fall
into the wrong hands, Mae. It's only safe in your hands."

"How can I stop them, they can take it surely?"

She shrugged, and I muttered how incredibly unhelpful
that was. She turned away. "Get some rest, Mae. I think
you're going to need it."

Her heels clacked away with the sharp angled form of
Mrs Cox replacing the image of Heather, the plump old
Kneel Woman. She turned at the door. "You and Tristram,
you were bonded by more than love." Her gaze was pierc-
ing. "It's blood that ties you."

Rest? Was she crazy? What did she mean blood? What
was there that was bigger than love? It wasn't a question I
could answer. Love wasn't something I could remember
feeling.

As I lay there, fiddling with the crisp cotton of the sheet
tucked around me I thought of something else.

Today I was eighteen.

Today was the day I could leave. When I'd arrived I'd
never wanted to come, but now I could leave of my own free
will... suddenly I didn't have anywhere I wanted to rush to.
I'd spent five days wandering in the past and it was five days
I'd missed spending with Phil and Tristan.

· · ·

I didn't have to stare at the ceiling by myself for long before the fall of footsteps pulled me from my puzzled thoughts.

Phil's hair was wild as she rushed into view. Tristan followed behind, his own golden skin pink with exertion. My heart stuttered when my eyes met his. "Guys, where the hell have you been?"

"Mae." Phil landed on the bed with a thump. "You should see what we've found."

"Well, don't keep me in suspense."

"All around the stones, we've found these stone soldiers, I've never seen anything like it."

"Really?" I pulled the sheet off my body, my eyes drifting to Tristan whose own gaze was settled on the skin of my legs. My blood warmed, my cheeks tinging pink, and I coughed to clear the obstruction sticking in my throat.

"Should you be up?" His own voice was deep and gravelly, and it only made the boiling of my blood bubble harder.

"Yes." I snapped.

He held his hands up, a chasing smirk flitting across his lips. "Okay, concerned individual backing down."

"Tell me everything." I grabbed at my pile of neatly folded clothes and darted behind the cotton hospital screen. I didn't know where the dress I'd come back through the stones with had gone. Probably a good thing I could slip into my own jeans and zipped hoodie. If I'd had to face the cotton dress I'd worn dripping wet, my brain may well have exploded over the walls.

"We were searching for anything that could explain where you were." Phil didn't meet my gaze and I glanced at Tristan.

"Didn't you tell her where I was?"

"Yes." His own gaze was wandering as he looked at anything other than me.

Phil's hesitation was palpable. For a girl who never stopped moving she was achingly still.

"You don't believe me." My stomach plummeted.

"The past, Mae? It's just not possible."

I straightened up. "Well, I stepped through the stones. I can remember every moment, every feeling." My gaze flicked to Tristan, remembering with desperate detail how wide the chasm was between Mae and Tristram. Yet they were going to die together... between when I was there and when they ended on the stones, they bonded with something other than love.

They still died.

My hand reached for his and even though he couldn't know the dark thoughts I contained, the miserable future we were living out in the past, his fingers wound into mine and gave a firm squeeze.

More than love...

"Show me the soldiers, maybe they will help me remember?"

"Remember what?" Phil's expression was etched with remorse and she smiled at me hopefully.

I grabbed her with my free hand and tugged her into my side. "It's okay. I know it's nuts."

"Hey, I'm all about the crazy, you know that."

"Better get on board the crazy train, my friend."

She grinned, letting out a deep sigh. "Boarding the train in three, two, one."

"Come on, show me the soldiers."

"I'm doing better than that. I was speaking to the cooks.

There is an old lady who lives in the village. She thinks she's a witch."

My heart boomed in my chest. Now wasn't the time to tell Phil if she wanted to be on my crazy train she'd have to accept the fact magic was real, and that I was a witch of some kind too.

"Then let's go break some rules and go find her."

Tristan's fingers squeezed mine. "I think you've broken all the rules."

I smiled at him, my blood warming again. *More than love.* "I'm a rule breaking Yank." *And a Druid priestess. And... who the hell knew what.*

We were passing out the dorm and I glanced back. This was the place everything changed. As I walked through I held myself straighter. It was time to find out who I was.

"I called Mum and Dad," Phil pulled me from my thoughts as the three of us trailed through the dark hallways. "They are coming back."

"What did you do that for?" I glanced at her.

"Mae, they've spent all their lives trying to find out what happened to this land. I couldn't not."

I shrugged. "I guess."

My eyes met Tristan's and we watched one another in the dim light. The past was the past. We may have ended our previous lives on those stones together, but this was our life now. And I wanted to know him, every part of him. The future, no matter how this turned out, was our chance to do just that.

We'd found one another again, and I had to believe it was for a reason. Fate, serendipity, whatever it was called.

"Let's go."

17

"Philomena Potts!" We turned, caught in the act of sneaking out the arched doorway. Mrs Barlow, the Romeo and Juliet fanatic was coming from the office.

"Just going for some fresh air." Phil hooked her hand through my elbow.

Mrs Barlow gave that wan smile all teachers specialise in when they are having trouble remembering who you are and don't really care because whatever they say goes. "Your friends can go get fresh air," she said, reinforcing my perception she didn't know who Tristan and I were. My gaze peeked at Tristan. She must be damn blind to not know who he was. As far as I could tell there wasn't a single person in the student body who looked quite like he did. Mrs Barlow fiddled with the pencil securing her greying bun. "Your parents have just called, Philomena, they're on their way from the airport." Sharp eyes travelled over Phil's dishevelled appearance. "I suggest you tidy up. We wouldn't want your parents thinking we don't take care of you, now, would we?"

"Heaven forbid." Phil's lips turned down at the edges and Mrs Barlow waddled off, her round backside swaying. "This isn't fair, why have they come so quick?"

I rolled my eyes and caught Tristan smirking. "Because you called them and told them you'd found ancient standing stones and an army made from the earth." As we'd walked the corridors, Tristan had filled me in on the rare and perfectly formed soldiers. I was torn between finding the village crazy who believed she was a witch, or seeing the soldiers.

"Still what did they do? Jump on the first flight they could get?"

I smiled at my friend and gave her an unexpected hug. She stiffened under my touch before relaxing and squeezing me back. "We won't do anything without you, I promise."

She was still pouting but turned back in the direction of the girl's wing. "Hey," she called back as she was about to push through the fire door.

"Yep?"

"No birthday kissing!" She grinned, and I blushed with the heat of the sun. I should have known she'd find out from my files. She probably knew my shoe size too.

Tristan's lips quirked at the edges, his dark gaze focused on my face. Thanks to Phil, all I could do now was stare at them and think about kissing.

"I'll keep that in mind." My eyes still focused on Tristan's lips. They smiled further until the cutest little dimple dipped in his cheek.

I closed my eyes, trying to access my memories. Had he always had a dimple? When I opened them, he was watching me with a dark, cryptic gaze.

"I'm glad you're here with me now." The words blurted from my mouth, but once they were out there I was relieved I'd said them. It was the truth. We may be strangers in this life, but I knew him deep down within me.

"I'm glad I don't want to kill you anymore."

"Me too." We watched one another for a moment. "Mrs Cox told me some stuff." I took a shuddering breath.

"Mrs Cox? She's a harpy of hell if ever there was one."

I grinned. "You know her—or at least you did. Heather?"

Tristan's burning coal eyes widened. "Wow, I didn't see that coming."

I shrugged. I didn't see any of this coming. "I can't believe this is real. It's all crazy, right?"

His fingers tangled with mine and he tugged me closer until his warm breath tickled the skin of my face. "Insane, Mae, but I know what I know, and I know you."

"Apparently, I hold the magic of the old ways." I shuddered another uneven breath. "There are others who want it. But I don't know how because I can't even feel anything."

His face hardened, the sumptuous turn of his lips settling into a hard line. "I will protect you from anything."

In a startling moment of clarity, the past made sense. He'd already protected me once. It was why we were both on the stones. Mrs Cox had said he wasn't meant to be there. "That's what worries me." I trembled deep down within the pit of my stomach. "What if this is an endless cycle, and the past happens all over again?"

He turned his face for the door, and the clouds and drizzle outside. "Only one way to find out."

I nodded. I wanted to kiss him. I wanted to hide in the moment and lose myself within the comforting presence he contained. But, instead I steeled myself. "Let's go find the village witch." I turned for the door, but his hand held mine, tugging me back. He reeled me closer, his lips swiftly grazing my mouth.

"Happy birthday." It was a low murmur and my stomach squeezed.

Our eyes met and I smiled. "Thank you."

We walked out into the darkening sky, me clutching the piece of paper Phil had got from the cook. As I glanced back, I was sure shadows moved within the draughty corners of the castle's entrance hall. I shivered and stepped closer to Tristan.

The cottage when we found it—down a stony road which looked like it hadn't changed in a hundred years—was run down. Dark ivy wrapped around the building as it did the castle. Tristan stepped up and knocked on the door. I hid behind his back, my hand pressed into the fabric of his t-shirt. I wanted to close my eyes and breathe in the fresh scent of sunshine and outdoors that clung to him, but the door opened.

I was expecting the *witch* to be an old woman, but the bright eyes of a woman in her thirties stared back at us. "Can I help?"

"Hi, sorry to bother you, but we are from the school." Tristan started, and I peeked from behind his back, bolstered by his words.

"I'm Mae." It was a simple statement. It contained so much. I was me, I was her. I was everything in between.

Tristan and I stared in shock as the woman fell to her knees. "Mae?"

"Uh, yeah. Hi." This was awkward. Tristan and I swapped confused looks.

"I always said you'd return. My Goddess."

I frowned. "Now steady on."

The woman lifted from the ground. "Please come in."

We followed her in, although the hairs were standing on the back of my neck. I had to remind myself we were looking for answers—any answers to any questions at this point.

"My liege," she dropped Tristan a small curtsey, and I snorted as his skin blushed.

"What's going on? How do you know who we are?" I stepped into the room. Bunches of herbs hung from low beams. They seemed oddly familiar and then I remembered my herb collection in my previous life, the aid and comfort I offered our people. "Are you a Druid?"

"Sheena," she offered her hand, her fingers trembling a little. I squeezed her fingers gently, hoping to put her at ease. I didn't know who she thought I was, but she didn't need to be scared. No one need fear me.

"No." Her face folded into a bitter mask. "Not the Druids they became. My family, we followed the old ways."

"But Druids don't exist, they are the old ways themselves." I knew this.

"No, they changed, hid, when you, when you..."

"Died," I prompted. Her eyes flit between mine and Tristan's.

"Yes. You took the power they were hoping to use."

"How do you know this? You're talking thousands of years." Was she a conduit too like Heather?

"Look." She motioned towards a collection of leather-bound books. They were ancient, their spines peeling and snapped. "My family have been keeping the records. We've never moved; always stayed here, waiting and hoping." Her hands wrung her apron in excitement.

"For two thousand years, you've been waiting?"

She nodded and gestured for us to sit on her floral chairs. I didn't want to sit, I wanted answers.

"How did your family know?"

"You healed our ancestor. You used your magic and thought she didn't know."

I tilted my head to the side and watched her silently.

"When you died she watched and waited. The power you had, it wasn't druid, it was stronger, fiercer, more powerful than anything. Then we all watched and waited."

"I don't have any power. Nothing."

Tristan's fingers reached for my shoulders and kneaded my tense flesh.

"Yet. Have you been heartbroken? Scared? It's inside you, it needs to awaken." Sheena pulled at her apron. Her face etched with fine lines and I guessed she was wishing the act of enlightenment hadn't fallen on her shoulders.

"My parents died. I think that's enough heartbreak for one lifetime."

She shook her head. "They weren't your parents, not really. This is where you belong." She glanced at Tristan, his fingers keeping contact with me at all times. "Family isn't always the blood you have, it's the blood you choose."

I stared at the ancient tomes on the shelf. "Can I look?"

"As much as you like. Can I offer you tea? Cake? Anything?"

I smiled, but it echoed with emptiness. "No, just time."

Sheena was disappointed. I guess she expected the moment, if it ever arrived, to go better. But I couldn't change the fact there wasn't a single thing magical about me. It was just the truth.

Maybe they were just dreams after all? Maybe this was all nonsense. Tristan came and took a book, perching his long legs against the shelf as he flipped the pages.

My head could speak any truth. But could my heart?

"What?" he asked. The dimple flashed.

"Nothing." But I wanted to tell him that nothing was everything and all things unknown were written in my heart.

"This is hopeless." I flung down the book. There were references to the growth of my power, as Sheena's ancestor recorded them. Myself and the liege had returned to the settlement one afternoon and from that point on Mary, the first recorder, noticed the change.

The records we were reading though weren't written until much later. Sheena had needed to translate some of the entries written in ancient Gaelic.

"We don't know what happened that afternoon to unlock her abilities."

Tristan's dark gaze settled on my face. "Your abilities?"

I wanted to stick my tongue out at him, but Sheena was watching me like she was expecting a miracle to spontaneously happen.

Screwing my eyes shut, I breathed slowly through my nose. 'I can't do this." I stood, abruptly scattering papers. In my haste, I knocked at a small table containing a vase. Water spilled over the floor as the glass crashed. "I'm sorry." I couldn't meet Sheena's gaze, couldn't meet the expectation she held for the person I'd never be.

My fingers pulled on the door handle, and I escaped out into the dark night. My hands shoved deep down into my pockets as I paced away, back down the lane.

"Mae, wait up." I turned to find Tristan jogging up behind me. I couldn't meet his gaze either, but he caught my hand, pulling me around to face him. "Don't run from me. Please?"

"Why? We don't even know each other. This is all crazy, stupid..." I struggled for a suitable word. "Shit."

He grinned, and I stared wordlessly at his face as the moon and stars shone on his white teeth and turned his golden hair into a pale silver. He turned my palm, planting a kiss on the sensitive skin before placing it over his heart. My own heart thrummed and raced. "Then it's shit we are in together."

"You died for me before. I won't allow that to happen again."

"Good, because I don't plan to allow history to repeat itself. If someone wants you, wants your magic, then we will fight them."

"I don't have magic, Tristram." It was an accident allowing his original name to slip from my lips and I dropped my gaze.

"You loved him." His gentle acknowledgement ached inside my chest.

"And you loved her."

"I only have the snapshots of the dreams, but yes, I did."

Silence spun a delicate web around us. I closed my eyes, lost some place between the past and the present. My feet wanted to run for the stones, to walk back through, to feel all that again. But my head told me to stay where I was. In *my* now. Here. With him.

"Mae," his words were a brush of air as his lips skimmed mine in the lightest of fluttering kisses. I gasped, my hands sliding along his chest, running from his heart to his throat to his hair. His lips found mine again, firmer and harder. I tasted his tongue as it teased the edge of mine.

His arms wound me in tight, cocooning me within his hold.

My heart banged against my chest.

Every fibre in my body tingled with scorching flames. He pecked kisses. "I'm glad we found one another again."

My eyes met his in the dark. "You really believe this, don't you?"

"I believe you."

"Even when I said I walked through the stones?"

"I know how I felt when you were missing. You weren't here, I couldn't feel you. The moment you came back I could sense where you were."

"More than love." I mumbled Mrs Cox's words.

"What did you say?"

His hands cupped my face. "More than love, it's what we are." My voice was louder, firmer than I would have thought possible.

He kissed the tip of my nose. "More than life, Mae."

"Let's go back to Fire Stone." I never thought I'd say those words. "We can see the books again tomorrow. Maybe it will all be clearer in the light of day."

He slipped his hand to mine, linking our fingers. So natural, yet so alien, all at once.

The school was dark when we approached up the sweeping drive. "It can't be that late, can it?"

I stepped up the worn stairs and a shiver passed over my skin. "Wait." I clutched Tristan's arm.

"What? We should get back before we get detention for the next hundred years."

"I can feel something." My skin prickled, a chill tensed

my stomach. I closed my eyes briefly, and within my veins a hum of golden energy coursed free and wild.

My eyes flew open. "I feel..." I hesitated to find the right words. Tristan turned and squinted at the forest.

"What's that? A fire?"

I followed his gaze, my stomach turning, my hand slipping from his grasp with cold sweat. "Come."

"Mae, no. I have to keep you safe." He tried to pull me back.

"No." A dark sensation of despair settled on my shoulders, pushing me down towards the earth. "Not this time."

I pulled on his hand dragging us towards the glow in the forest. Sadly, I knew what we would find. I could see it before we even reached the scene. Within my mind's eye the trees sent me the images. I could make out the shapes in white robes, the startling fire and...

"Phil," I screeched as we ran into the clearing with the stones. From under the white-robed hoods murmurs lifted into the air. I couldn't hear them clear enough, couldn't work out what they were asking for. "Father?" I blinked up at Mae's father. There he was, and not a day older than when I'd seen him last on my trip through the past. Next to him, with hair as bright at starlight was the woman I'd seen in my vision before I'd come back to Fire Stone.

"Mae." This was the woman who'd marched through settlements full of women and children in her search for me, destroying everything in her path.

My breath hitched. Tristan tried to plant himself in front of me, but I wouldn't let him. Phil stared at me with wild eyes. Tied onto the stones she was in the spot where Tristram and Mae's bones had settled for thousands of years. Her eyes leaked droplets of water down her cheeks and onto the rough grey stone.

"All you need is a little nudge, Mae." The woman with the silver hair said. "Then we can pick up where we left off."

"No. I don't have any magic; there is nothing there."

I was lying though. Within my veins the golden fluid river of energy rushed into every cell. I had no clue what to do with it though.

"Of course, you do." The woman with the silver hair and smooth skin stepped closer. "We've been waiting a long time to get it."

"Mum," Phil managed to squeak from under her gag, but the woman didn't turn. I was going to be sick.

"I don't have anything that's any use to you. Nothing. I'm just a girl from Queens."

In slow motion Mae's father lifted a jewelled dagger and thrust it into Phil's chest. I screamed but no sound came out as I crumpled to the floor, watching blood run from my friend onto the stones.

"This was all you and him." The woman pointed between me and Tristan. "If you hadn't ruined our plans all those years ago this would never have happened."

I crawled forward, ignoring her words. My hand slipped in a river of Phil's blood. Her eyes were vacant as they stared at the sky.

A burning rampage coiled within my body. My legs trembled, my hands shook. The earth rumbled under my knees.

I grabbed the blade from her chest, gripping it firmly in my palm. It slid from between her ribs with more ease than I was expecting. With a slash, I swiped it across my palm, mingling our blood.

The Druid priest and his evil sidekick watched laughing as I stumbled from the ground. "You don't know what you're doing," he scorned. The gathering of Druids lowered their hoods and I exhaled sharply as I saw all the teachers from Fire Stone. Was this whole place about me—about me getting my magic and wielding it?

Ignoring him, I stepped for Tristan. Under the moon his face was pale, his eyes sought mine. "Mae?"

"I'm going to discover my magic." I brushed my lips against his cheek.

"You can't. You will die. You died on the stones. We both did."

I shook my head. Picking his hand in mine, I cut across his skin with the blade and he hissed. I gripped our palms together tight, meshing my bloody hand with his. Mixing Phil's blood with both of ours. "They won't know who I am. I'll have the upper hand. The only place for me to learn is back then, back when magic was normal." The two of them stepped closer, clearly our time was up. Tristan gasped as he glanced at the ground. Where our blood had dropped blooms of purple sprouted from the earth.

"Don't try to save me this time. It's the only way we will live."

He shook his head. "You need to tell that to me two thousand years ago, because I think it's in my blood to save you."

"More than love." I smiled, but it was watery. "I'll tell you."

I went to turn away, ready to run for the past, but he gripped me tight. "How will you know who you are? You aren't prepared, you can't just go time walking."

"How do I know anything, Tristan? I don't, but at the same time I do." Time was running out. The circle of Druids drew closer. "If I stay here, we die, again." I clutched at him in one brief moment of weakness. "I have something they want; how can I stop them if I don't know what it is?" I whispered into his ear. After the briefest of pauses he nodded, the skin of his cheek grazing mine. I turned and faced Phil's lifeless form. "Give her a real burial, Tristan." I didn't give him time to answer as I ran for the stones, placing my hands towards them. A deep crack met my touch and behind me a shout lifted through the air.

The stones were mine. It was what Mae's father had never realised, but the one thing I knew above anything else.

Whoever I was, and whatever I contained, the stones would always connect me to the things I loved. I glanced back as the image of the future faded. Tristan was watching me, and my heart pounded.

"Curse the land." The cry went through the air as the vision of the future evaporated.

It didn't matter. They could curse what they liked. By the time I'd finished, there would be no breath left in their bodies for them to curse us with.

To be continued ... *The Realm of Bone and Dust*
June 17th 2019

Ⅱ

Join Anna's Magical Hangout to find out more!
https://www.facebook.com/groups/286953915073566/

ACKNOWLEDGMENTS

This book has been lurking on my computer for nearly a year. I fell in love with Tristram and Mae when I initially wrote their story in a novella for an anthology. They swept me away with their magic and I was desperate to know where I could help them go. This book is the first step in that journey.

My thanks go to Lianne, Nikki and Andrea who all in their way helped me shine this into something wonderful.

My special thanks to Leah, if you tell me you love it then I know I've done something right?

To my family. I love you.

To my readers I thank you and love you from the bottom of my heart.

I shall see you all in the Realm of Bone and Dust.

Anna
   Surrey, UK

ABOUT THE AUTHOR

A book hoarder and coffee addict by heart Anna Bloom loves to write extraordinary stories about real love. Based south of London with her husband, three children and a dog with a beard, Anna likes to connect with readers, fan girl over her favourite authors and binge watch Supernatural while drinking lots of wine.

ALSO BY A B BLOOM

Gravity YA Fantasy (The Complete Boxset)

Gone YA Mature Contemporary Romance

Made in the USA
Columbia, SC
05 December 2023

27797963R00130